Element
of
Surprise II
The Continuation
By: Mr. Ish

The accomplishment of this book is dedicated to my son Isaiah

Copyright © 2020 by Mr. Ish All rights reserved.

Author: Mr. Ish
Publisher: Mr. Ish
ISBN No: 978-1-7351276-0-6
LCCN No: TBA
Editing: Mr. Ish
Typesetting: Elicia Hughes

Element of Surprise: The Continuation is a work of fiction. Names, characters, places, and incidents are the products of the author's imagination or are used fictitiously. Any resemblance to actual events, locales, or persons, living or dead, is entirely coincidental.

Chapter 1

Five days left for Adonis

Mikros went back to his desk. He was furious that the Captain instructed him to stand down. "Stupid fucking asshole," he stated as he plopped down in his chair. Its been fifteen years since Travis Owens was murdered in cold blood, and up until now, there weren't any leads. Still, Mikros was told not to follow up. His frustrations were paramount. He sat in his chair looking downright disgusted. Then suddenly the Captain appeared.

"Mikros," the Captain called out, motioning for him to come back to his office.

With the attitude of a scorn bitch, he got up and made his way to the Captains' office.

"Have a seat and stop looking so fucking pitiful," the Captain barked just as he entered.

Mikros sat down and tried to change his facial expression, but it still labored with defeat.

"Look here Mikros, go ahead and pursue your leads and handle things the way you see fit." The Captain leaned forward across the desk then continued, "But I'm telling you now, Michael Owens isn't to have any relief from any of this," he stated with a pointing finger before sitting back in his chair. "Now tell me what you have," he said more calmly.

A smile of delight grew fast across Mikros face. He got excited as hell. "Well—

"Whoa-whoa. Stop it with the feminine shit. Express yourself like a fucking man," the Captain interrupted with sternness. He hated when Mikros behaved in such a manner.

Mikros cleared his throat. "Well first of all, I finally found out who Chaz is? Her name is Chantell Davis. She's the adopted sister of a guy named Adonis Davis. Which happen to be the man responsible for the murder of Travis Owens, Michael's little brother. But I doubt that Michael had any knowledge of this. If so, I'm pretty sure Chantell would have been killed a long time ago."

The Captain gave him an impressed gaze. "Alright, what else?" he asked.

"That's it, that's all I have right now. Oh yeah, I almost forgot. Adonis Davis is in prison up in New Jersey, and he's scheduled for release in five days. If I drop the warrant on him now, I could fly there and pick him up before his release. If I'm lucky I'll catch Chantell as well."

The Captain began tapping his index finger on the desk. His eyes shifted as if he was in deep thought. "Yeah, go ahead and drop the warrant on Mr. Davis. But as it stands, we're gonna have to clear Chantell as a suspect since we have Michael taking the hit for all those murders. And did you charge him with Kleins and Wiggins as well?"

"I charged Michael Owens with everything I could think of. Except the bodies of the two women that were found in the trunk of his car. I'm still waiting on their identification before I can complete the paperwork. It's kind of hard to identify decapitated victims."

"Alright then, I guess it's settled. Have Sykes put together a press release that will clear Chantell as a suspect while you drop the warrant on her brother," the Captain concluded.

"I'll get right on it," Mikros said then left.

***

Detective Erica Sykes was standing in the hallway at the vending machine when Mikros crept up behind her. "Girl, you are the only woman that has ever had me thinking about going straight," Mikros told her in a rare manly voice.

Sykes turned around smiling. Her cinnamon brown complexion and long, silky black hair—which draped over her shoulders— seemingly glowed. She was by far the sexiest woman on the Atlanta police force. Not to mention, she possessed a mouthwatering thickness. It didn't matter what angle she stood at, her ass and hips were always on display. The bitch was bad. Though she stood only five foot two, her whopping beauty soared to great heights.

"Oh, Mikros please, you ain't thinking 'bout nothing but a nine. And I ain't talking about a gun," she replied.

"But of course you are," he shot back while fanning his hand.

The two of them shared a few giggles before getting back to business. "What's up Mikros, what kind of sideways favor do you want now?" she asked, grabbing her bottle of water from the machine.

"Not me, the Captain. Since I have to drop a warrant on a suspect, the Captain wants you to compose a press release to clear the lady we thought was a suspect."

Erica twisted the top off her water bottle, took a sip, then asked, "What lady, and a suspect for what?"

"Remember all the chaos surrounding the murders and arsons that were going on a few weeks ago."

"Oh yeah, that crazy case that drove Kleins off the deep end."

"Right, but not exactly. It's a lot of shit with that. Basically, Kleins was helping Michael Owens frame the girl Chaz, aka Chantell

3

Davis. But anyway, she's in the clear now so that's why the Captain wants that press release."

"Yeah, okay just give me a summary of what needs to be explained and I'll put it together," she informed as she stepped off.

Mikros couldn't help but gawk at her ass as she walked down the corridor, thinking to himself, *why I had to be gay.*

Chapter 2
Jersey City, NJ

Rep pulled up and parked his Jeep across the street from his resting quarters. He had been living in the building on the corner of Grant Ave and Bergen Ave for over ten years. Although his apartment was more of a bachelor's pad than a residence, he still managed to keep the spot up to par. Credited to the THOT bitch—Monique—who he had staying with him. He made sure she earned her keep.

Rep could smell the sweet aroma of Monique's cooking the minute he opened the door. She was a beast at cheffing it up in the kitchen.

"Baby, that's you?" she yelled out after hearing the door shut.

"This bitch bugging with that baby shit," he mumbled. "Yeah!" he replied as he kicked off his Timbs by the door.

Monique entered the living room wearing next to nothing. She had on a black tee shirt, that's it. Nothing covering her lower region, not even panties.

"I'm making spaghetti with my special sauce," she bragged happily.

"Um, yummy, now move out my way," he stated coldly as he walked past her heading towards the shower.

Monique squinted her eyes with attitude. She hated how he treated her at times.

"Rep, why you gotta act like that towards me?" she questioned as she followed behind him.

He chuckled to himself stopping short of the bathroom door. When he turned around she was dead up on him. "Yo, backup." He pushed her back gently. "First of all, you ain't my woman. Secondly, we have an agreement." He began counting off their terms on his fingers. "I fuck you! You suck me! And you keep the apartment clean. We ain't lovers, in a relationship, or none of that. I said that you could stay here rent-free under those conditions, and you agreed." His eyes got big. "Now all of a sudden you calling me baby, talking 'bout you love me. Naw ma, we ain't 'bout to do that." He walked in the bathroom and slammed the door before she could respond.

Her face took a dive so to speak. He really made her feel like shit. Just when she was about to step off, he swung the door back open.

"See, this some bullshit, you done got my dick hard. Get in here and bend over!"

Her frown turned into a tight-lipped smirk. He was subconsciously the master of sending mixed messages. In turn, having her acting as if they were a couple. Moreover, she wasted no time in strutting her skinny ass in that bathroom. She was excellent at being a cum bucket. Right there at Rep's every beck and call.

Monique bent over and put one leg up on the tub, using the sink to brace herself. The sight of her nicely shaved protruding pussy got his hormones raging. He dropped his pants, allowing for his dick to maximize its blood flow. He stepped in gripping his shaft at the base and smacking it against her throbbing cunt.

She began to hiss blissfully as her pussy got wet.

Then he started to probe her slit until he gained access to her sweetness. That's when shit got real. He grabbed her waist and slid up in her. Followed by a hard, strong thrust.

"No, stop!" She screamed damn near jumping in the sink.

Rep pulled out and started laughing. "How you supposed to be in house pussy, but every time I fuck you, you be tryna run out the house," he managed to say while giggling.

"Fuck you, Rep. You did that shit on purpose. Move!" she shouted, pushing him out her way and storming out.

"Oh, hell no!" he yelled trailing her with a semi hard on. "You gotta make this motherfucker spit. I need that nut."

She wasn't trying to hear it. She went back in the kitchen to finish cooking.

Rep crept up behind her, palming her ass while kissing her gently on the neck. "My bad. Come on, let's finish," he whispered as she stirred the sauce.

She tried to resist, but the whore within wouldn't allow it. She sighed. "Alright, but I'm getting on top," she said with a smile.

By the time she turned around he was lying on the kitchen floor stroking his dick. "Well, what you waiting for?"

The thought of him being an asshole crossed her mind. Slowly, she lowered herself onto his member. "Ohhh," she moaned with her eyes closed. And the minute his dick disappeared inside of her, he was busting off. She could feel his sperm skeet up in her. "No!" she shouted as if that was gonna stop him from cuming. He grabbed her by the waist and wiggled his hips until his balls were empty.

She got up angry as ever. "You selfish as hell," she said seriously upset.

"What I do?" he asked while laughing.

"You know what you did," she snapped as she went over to the stove.

He got up off the floor. "You could be mad all you want. Just make sure you clean your pussy before you finish cooking my food," he said before going to the shower.

Element of Surprise II

***

All Monique could think about as she cooked was, how much she was falling in love with Rep. Even though she knew he wasn't the right kind of dude for her. Still, she couldn't control her heart. She didn't mind being talked down to, disrespected, or fucked like a three-dollar hoe. As long as he showed interest in her, she accepted whatever came with it. Ironically, it was his—fuck you bitch—demeanor that really turned her on. Yeah, her whole perception of what love is had been distorted.

After making Rep's plate she sat it on the stove. Then she put on some music and started to roll his post-meal blunt. She loved catering to him.

Rep walked out the bathroom wearing only water. He stormed over to the stereo and shut it off. "You tryna be funny. I told you don't be playing that Jadakiss shit up in here. I'm tired of motherfuckers saying I look like that nigga. Don't put that shit on while I'm in here," he dictated then stormed back into the bathroom.

After dinner, they sat on the couch sharing a blunt and quality time. It was as if they were really an item. At least in Monique's mind anyway.

"You know you got some iron lungs. How you gon' be that skinny with lungs that strong?" he asked her jokingly.

She handed him the blunt, exhaling. "A'ight, now don't get mad when I start talking about the Lox coming out with a new album."

He started laughing so hard he began choking. After he caught his breath, he looked up at her. She was having a field day at his expense. It was obvious that they were high as hell.

Rep dudded the blunt out and left it in the ashtray. Then he scooped Monique up and tossed her over his shoulder. She screamed playfully. He took her in the bedroom and tossed her on the bed. "You got jokes right," he said, climbing on top of her. When their eyes met all laughter subsided. Her gaze held a sincere craving to be sexually satisfied. She wanted him to make love to her.

"Rep," she whispered seductively, "I love you."

"Damn!" he scoffed, raising up off her. "Why the fuck you always gotta say some stupid shit to fuck my high up." He bolted out and went in the living room to watch TV.

"Why the fuck you always gotta be so cold and heartless," She retorted in pursuit of him.

He responded by taking the remote off the table and plopping down on the couch.

"You tryna be all macho and shit, like my pussy's trash or something. I do everything for you. Everything!" she yelled in frustration.

He cracked a smile. "We got an agreement," he said coldly as he clicked on the TV.

"Fuck that agreement. I'm falling in love with you, and you gon' love me back," she said matter-of-factly. Then she sat down next to him. "Rep look," her voice got calmer. "If you were gonna be this way towards me, you should have never started fucking with me."

He looked at her like she was crazy. "Girl, did you forget you use to be a hoe?"

"Fuck you nigga!" she shouted in his face then ran in the room.

He couldn't help but enjoy the way he was making her squirm for his love. "I wish Qua was here to see this shit," he said to himself. "Oh shit!" He jumped up, remembering he had to send Qua those pictures of Chaz. "Monique!" he called out.

"Eat my ass nigga!" she yelled back.

He started laughing. "Girl, come here."

"Wait..." Within seconds she was in the living room. "What? What can I do for you mister heartless?"

"I need you to print these pictures out for me so I could send 'em to Qua." He handed her his phone.

"Yeah, I guess a hoe good for something." She snatched his phone and sat down at the computer.

"You know I fucks with you," Rep smiled.

Chapter 3

Fulton County Jail,

Atlanta, GA

Flex sat shackled to a chair, listening to the jail's Psychiatrist ramble on about a bunch of nothing. The short Asian man sat behind his desk asking all types of off the wall questions. But Flex never answered. His interest in what the Doctor asked didn't exist.

"Mr. Owens, it's very imperative that you answer at least the key questions if you wanna get off suicide watch. Now I understand that you're angry and faced with a multitude of serious charges. But I believe you're ready to return to general population. So, if you want me to authorize your release from that padded room, I suggest you start talking."

Flex looked at the Doctor like he wanted to spit in his face. A light chuckle escaped him. "Doc, listen here. I ain't got no problem talking to you about how I feel or what's on my mind. But the type of questions you're asking me don't make sense." He leaned forward. "What does the kind of gas I put in my car got to do with anything. Just ask me the relevant questions. Stop it with all that tryna get to know me shit. You here to do your job and receive a check. Stop acting like you're really concerned about a motherfucker," he expressed angrily.

"Well now we're making progress. You're right Mr. Owens. I don't give a fuck about you. Should I? Of course not. Because you're a fucking low life and I'm an educated man who lives his life according to the civilized ways of humanity. Which by the way, has nothing to do with the fact that I look down on individuals that aren't in my social arena. So, here's what I'm prepared to do for you. Answer five questions and I'll send your black ass back to general population with the rest of the animals and scumbags," the Doctor expressed calmly.

The stunned look on Flex's face showed his disbelief. "You funny as hell. You funny to the point that I wish these cuffs wasn't on me so I could beat the fuck out of you. But since I can't show you how much I appreciate your humor, I guess I'll answer your questions so I could return to the jungle with the rest of the animals."

"What a delight," the Doc responded grabbing his pen.

About forty minutes later Flex was cleared to return to general population. After placing his belongings in his cell, he sought out the unit's barber for a haircut. He approached the barber while he was in the process of cutting another inmate's hair. Kind of timidly, Flex asked if there was someone next in line for a haircut. The barber said no. But when the barber got done he put the clippers down and walked off.

"Yo, I asked you to cut my hair. Where you going?" Flex inquired.

"Nigga, you got commissary? 'Cause that's the only way I'ma cut your hair. You gotta pay for that, haircuts are luxuries 'round here." The guy stated then stepped off.

Flex gave the man a dirty look as he walked away. "Fuck it, I'll cut my own shit," he said then grabbed the clippers. About fifteen minutes later, he had a bald head and goatee. It was the only style he knew how to do. Not to mention, the shit didn't look bad. Flex stared in the mirror, admiring his new look. The bald look suited him better anyway. He looked more like a gangster now. "Yeah, word," he said rubbing his head before heading towards the shower.

When he made it back to his cell there was a bag of commissary on his bunk. Skeptically, he looked at the bag. He was no fool, he heard stories about how booty bandits reeled jokers in with snacks and food. He threw his towel down and put on his sneakers. But before he could address the tier about the bag, the barber came to his cell.

"Yo, pardon me homeboy," the barber said with his hands up symbolizing peace.

"What's up?" Flex responded aggressively. He was ready for whatever.

"Naw big dawg, it ain't like that. Pike sent that bag up here for you. I sat it in here 'cause you was in the shower," the barber explained.

Flex peeped that the dude wasn't the same arrogant bastard he encountered earlier. He smiled internally as he stared the guy down. "Yeah well, next time you got something for me, hold it. Don't just be walking all up in my shit."

"I respect that. They call me New York." New York extended his hand.

"Flex," he retorted, accepting the gesture of goodwill.

"Oh yeah, my bad about earlier. It's just niggas be on some other shit."

"Naw, I understand. You gotta get ya hustle on. Ain't nothing wrong with that. But'um, I'm 'bout to get myself together so I'll holla at you later."

"True dat," replied New York walking off.

Once Flex finished grooming himself and putting the food away that Pike sent him, he relaxed on his bunk. He laid there thinking about how he went from being in a position of power, to being controlled by the system. Never in his lifetime did he imagine being stripped of his ghetto fabulous status, to endure the tragedies of being just another statistic. This wasn't what he had planned for his life by far. In a blink of an eye, he went from king to convict. No lawyer, no one to come visit, and no one he could trust. Berry's face jumped into his head, followed by Mack then Tay. "Fuck!" he said in frustration as he sat up. He became angry with himself. "How could I be so fucking stupid," he questioned while rubbing his head.

The sound of the C.O. stopping by his cell prompted him to stand. Then a letter slid under his cell door. "Mommy," he said, reading the sender's name as he picked up the envelope. He was baffled. He hadn't heard from or seen his mother in about a year and a half. The last time they were in each other's presence, Flex was pistol whipping one of his runners for tricking off with her. Ultimately, leading to the young nigga's demise. And he made his mother watch.

Overwhelmed by emotion, he eagerly ripped the envelope open and snatched the letter out.

Dear Michael, he started to read as he sat down on his bunk.

I know you weren't expecting to hear from me. However, I just returned from rehab. I've been in the program since the last time I saw you. Michael, I know you may despise me or even hate me. But I'm still your mother and I really do love you. I'm truly sorry for my actions and I'm asking you to forgive me. Please Michael, I beg of you. A lot of the things that I have done in the past may not be easy to forgive me for. I'm hoping in time, you'll find it in your heart to do so. There isn't nothing in this world that I wouldn't do to mend the damages between us.

I heard what happen with Norris and in a sense, I blame myself for that as well. He was a good man and he didn't deserve to leave the way he did. As of now, I'm working on finding a job and a good church to attend. My phone number is on the back. Please, give me a call and put my name on your visiting list.

I love you,
Mom!

Tears of joy began to spot the letter as they fell from Flex's face. He was happy to hear that his mother was clean. "I forgive you mommy. I forgive you," he managed to sob out as he cried vigorously.

"Prepare for chow!" Yelled the C.O. before popping open the cell doors.

Quickly, Flex moved to get himself together. The last thing he needed was for a bunch of hardened criminals to witness him having an emotional breakdown.

New York showed up at his cell. "Yo, you coming out for dinner?" he asked as if they were buddies or something.

"Yeah I'm coming. Give me a minute," Flex responded, tucking the letter inside his sock. The fellas made their way over to get their tray. Afterwards, they copped a seat at the first available table.

Silently, Flex sat there picking through his food. It was obvious that he was in deep thought. Apparently, that letter was still affecting him.

"Yo son, you a'ight?" New York wanted to know.

"I'm good. I just got some stuff on my mind that's all. But'um, let me ask you a question, how could get a letter to Pike?"

"That shouldn't be too hard. Pike comes up here every night after lockdown to make sure all the showers are cleaned. He got a lot of juice with the guards. Pike the man 'round here. Shit, pretty soon you ain't gone have to lock in at all, except at night. Pike already got the word out that you was his uncle."

Flex marveled at how much respect Pike had for him. He attempted to smile but caught himself. He felt it was necessary to maintain a stern disposition. He didn't want to send the wrong message, especially while being housed on a max tier with other murderers. "I'm just glad to be back in the regular population. That padded room is a motherfucker."

Before New York could respond, the C.O. called out that chow was over. Slowly, everybody began to dump their trays, squeezing in the last of their conversations. It was about 6:30 pm and the night was over.

"A'ight Flex, I'll get up with you in the morning at breakfast," stated New York giving him dap.

"Yeah, next day."

The second Flex stepped inside his cell, the electrical steel door slid shut. Those country ass guards ain't waste no time in locking the inmates down. He sat on his bunk and retrieved the letter from his sock. He wanted to read it again. That letter was the only temporary relief he had.

After reading the letter, he laid down cloaked in the memories of him and his mother having fun together. Memories of the old days made him feel good. Then he drifted off to sleep.

"Mike, come on. Let's go to the pool," his little brother Travis called out as he pulled on Flex's arm.

A warm pleasant smile blessed his sleeping face. Suddenly, his dream transformed into a nightmare. Flashes of Travis laying in a coffin removed his smile. Images of his mother deteriorating right before his eyes caused him to start twitching. "Ahh!" Flex sat up, sweating and breathing hard. He looked around, no one else was in the cell. Yet, he felt a presence in his company. "Please Lord, give me the strength to make it through the night?" he asked out loud as he got up out his bunk and went to the sink. That's when he noticed Pike standing at his cell door laughing.

The cell door opened. "Come on, bro. I wanna introduce you to somebody."

Pike ushered Flex over to the booth where Ms. Wallace awaited. She was the guard in charge of overseeing the trusties and escorting them to and from their designated work areas. And Pike was definitely her biggest fan. Not because she was the baddest bitch in the building. 'Cause that was not the case. If anything, she was average at best. Brown skin, cute face and thick. But the fact that she was a correctional officer is what really turned him on. That, and the fact that she was a big flirt.

"Ms. Wallace, this my Uncle Michael, the one I was telling you about."

As Pike expected, Ms. Wallace flashed her enticing smile, working her eyes. "Uhm, I heard a lot about you, Mr. Michael Owens," she said with a lisp.

"How do you do ma'am," Flex retorted. Trying to sound as if he wasn't a drug dealing, gun slinging, murderous motherfucker.

Ms. Wallace waved her hand, "Boy it ain't no need in tryna sound all respectful. Everybody 'round here know what type of crazy nigga you is. But on the strength of Pike," she smiled, "Ima put you in charge of keeping this unit clean. At least you'll be out your cell most of the day. That's the best I could do for you, being as though you on a max tier."

"A'ight word. I really appreciate that, Ms. Wallace," Flex expressed, nodding his head up and down.

"Uhm... Well, just don't fuck it up. Now y'all got about five minutes to talk 'cause they gone call count up in a minute." As she strutted back in the booth Pike couldn't help but keep his eyes trained on her butt, thinking to himself how he'd love to suck a fart out her ass.

Chapter 4
Patty-Mae's house
Jersey City, NJ

Since Dee-Dee's run-in with the sheriff officers at the mall, her and Chaz had been laying low. Neither of them stepped a foot out that house. Initially, they contemplated leaving and relocating until Adonis got out. But after further assessing their circumstances, they figured it didn't make sense to leave and take unnecessary risks. Especially since they were already in a good location. Also, the one-hundred and six thousand dollars from Patty-Mae's stash, was too much money to be lugging around. It just made more sense for them to stay put.

Dee-Dee was in the middle of taking a shit when she heard Chaz scream. She jumped up, with shit wedged in the crack of her ass, she ran to check on her. When she got to the room Chaz was sitting with her hands covering her mouth and eyes glued to the TV.

Dee-Dee was about to speak but the obvious pushed her to hone in on the TV as well. In the upper left corner of the screen, Chaz's picture and her real name was being featured. Inquisitively, the women watched on as the Captain of the Atlanta Police Department held a live press conference.

"A few weeks ago, we aired a special about a young lady that we believed to have been involved in a series of slayings about our community." The Captain stopped to clear his throat. "However, after combing through the evidence and thoroughly paying attention to the facts, I am hereby recalling all warrants on Chantell 'Chaz' Davis and relinquishing her as a suspect in any crimes pertaining to the case at hand. Furthermore, I would like to extend my deepest apologies to Chantell and her family."

Although the Captain continued to talk, Chaz tuned him out. She heard what she needed to hear. She jumped up off the bed, ecstatic. She couldn't believe it. Finally, the bullshit was over.

Her and Dee-Dee grabbed hands and started jumping around in a circle. High praises for Chaz being in the clear showed joyously as they danced. Then Chaz felt something mushy underneath her foot. Abruptly, she stopped jumping and turned her face up. "Ill! What the fuck is that?" she questioned authoritatively as she took notice of the dooky she stepped in.

Dee-Dee gave her the dumbest look ever. "You had me thinking something happened, so I ran in here right off the toilet."

"Get this shit off my foot!" Chaz yelled in a tantrum.

***

About thirty minutes later, the ladies had showered and gotten dressed. They intended on celebrating to the fullest. Neither had a specific thing in mind, but they were definitely going to enjoy themselves.

Chaz stood in the mirror lusting over her reflection. The way those jeans hugged her curves made her ass look delicious. She so wished she had a clone to make love to. "These jeans do look good, but this ugly ass shirt gotta go," she said pulling the blouse off. Then she admired her exposed breast, which sat up perfectly without a bra.

"I should rock out like this," she giggled to herself. She snatched up a blue V-neck tee shirt and tossed it on. And of course, her nipples protruded tastefully.

"Perfect," she said, giving herself a sexy smile.

"Bitch don't play with me. You better put a bra on," expressed Dee-Dee as she tied her sneakers.

Like an upset child, Chaz stomped her foot and sighed, "Oh boy, why you always gotta act like that. You mad jealous for no reason."

"It got nothing to do with being jealous. But we went through hell tryna clear ya name, and now you wanna go from being a gangsta to a porn star. Save that shit for the bedroom."

Chaz was in the process of responding when Rep unexpectedly keyed his way into the house and began calling out for Dee-Dee.

"Upstairs!" she yelled. "Now all of a sudden this nigga wanna come by," she said to Chaz.

"That's your brother." Chaz pointed at her.

Rep entered the room just as the ladies were putting the finishing touches on their outfits. He wore a collective smile, conveying how pleased he was with the trending topic of Chaz being cleared. "Okay sis, I see your girl Chaz done wiggled her way out of all that drama," he stated animatedly.

Infectious smiles spread wide across their faces. Chaz brushed her shoulders off like it was nothing. As if to say, "That shit wasn't about nothing." Then she actually said it. "That shit wasn't about nothing. I just had to stay low key until they figured out that I ain't do shit." She shot Dee-Dee a conniving look.

"A'ight. Well, I know y'all gon' hit the town and turn up, so just give me a call when y'all available," Rep stated.

Dee-Dee looked at him like—what the fuck we gon' call you for. "Yeah, whatever." she said rolling her eyes. She wasn't stupid, she knew Rep was tryna swindle his way into Chaz's pants. There was no way she would ever trust him around any of her bitches, especially Chaz.

Chaz noted the change in Dee-Dee's body language. She could tell that Rep's comment rubbed her the wrong way. So, just to fuck with her, she walked up in Rep's personal space. "Yeah, we'll call you," she said sensually while batting her eyes.

Before Rep could capture a full smile Dee-Dee wedged between them. "Bitch, stop playing with me." Her eyes went cold and her tone turned venomous.

Rep chuckled. He knew Dee-Dee was in her feelings. "Sis, I'ma holla at you later."

"Deuces!" Dee-Dee responded bitterly.

He shook his head with a smile. He wasn't beat for her bullshit. "Oh yeah, when the hell is Ms. Mae coming back. She ain't usually gone this long. I been calling her phone, but it's off. When was the last time you spoke to her?" he inquired out of concern.

"I talked to her last night and she'll be back next week. Now get the fuck out. Come on, you gotta go." She started pushing him out the room.

"Get the fuck off me." He snatched away, contorting his face distastefully. "Stupid bitch," he mumbled as he walked out the room and down the stairs to leave.

Chaz stood there struggling not to laugh.

"Don't make me fuck you up!" Dee- Dee spat angrily.

***

Chaz walked out on the porch and took a big breath of fresh air. Slowly, she exhaled while stretching her arms towards the sky. "I'm free," she whispered. "Free!" she screamed.

"Oh please, get in the car. You doing too much." Dee-Dee pushed past her heading towards the car.

"Awe, my baby still mad," Chaz replied as she skipped down the stairs and got in the Buick. She was so happy to be cleared, she didn't know what to do. After getting in the car, she started doing a bunch of silly shit: rubbing the dashboard, opening the glove compartment. Then she started playing with the windows.

"Stop! Stop! You act like you ain't never been in a fucking car before. Sitting up here acting retarded." Dee-Dee started the car and drove off.

Without a rebuttal, Chaz got a grip on herself and began staring out the window, Thoughtlessly, she watched on as society continued to move about. Cars, people, animals, and even the trees felt good to look at. She never realized how much she took her freedom for granted until it hung in the balance of being taken away. In those moments, she understood a valuable lesson in appreciating life. Thoughts of one day becoming a mother slithered its way into her head. She smiled as Dee-Dee drove past a mother—hand in hand—with her son. Having a family with Adonis was something she longed for, for years. But then her joyous thoughts suddenly disappeared, replaced by the soul snatching flashbacks of her uncle Tyrone robbing her of her innocence when she was a little girl. The horrific images of him molesting her filled her with rage. Tears of shame, hurt and revenge scrolled freely from her previously bright, but now dark with hatred eyes. Everything went blank. Her mind didn't compute anything but pain.

By this time, Dee-Dee had pulled into the parking lot of Applebee's and parked. Chaz didn't even realize it. Nor was she paying attention that Dee-Dee had been talking to her for the past two minutes.

"So, you just gonna ignore me and stare out the window, huh?" Dee-Dee asked agitated.

"Huh, oh, what you say?" inquired Chaz, wiping the tears from her face before turning from the window.

"I know you ain't sitting up here crying?" Dee-Dee asked, shocked.

"Bitch, you'd be crying to if you was just cleared for multiple homicides. And why the fuck did you come to AppleBee's in Newark. You could have at least gone to the one on Route 22."

Dee-Dee started laughing, "Girl you know you a celebrity now, ain't nothing like coming back to your roots and getting the home crowd involved," she said exiting the car.

"I heard that hot shit," Chaz happily stated as she followed suit.

The minute they entered AppleBee's motherfuckers got to whispering, nudging one another and pointing in their direction. One man even blurted out, "Ain't that the girl Chaz they just dismissed those murder charges against." And when he said that, people really started taking notice.

Chaz was doing her best not to lose her mind from all the notoriety. It was hard though.

Dee-Dee stood off to the side wearing the biggest smile ever. She was really loving the moment. It made her feel like she was the one in the limelight.

Smilingly, the ladies took a seat at the bar. Then unexpectedly three young ladies approached and asked Chaz for her autograph. Wow...thought Chaz, as she signed her name, followed by A.K.A. Chantell Davis.

"If it's not too much trouble can we have a picture with you," asked one of the young ladies.

"Yeah, none of your bloggers would ever believe that we met you, unless we had proof," another girl chimed in.

Chaz and Dee-Dee gave each other a skeptical look. "What do you mean bloggers?" Chaz asked curiously.

"Here look." One of the girls pulled up a webpage on her Galaxy cell phone and handed it to Chaz for her to see. She had a mean following. Something like an A-list celebrity. People had been leaving comments left and right. Such as, "Chaz is the baddest bitch in every sense of the word." And another person commented, "She even got me thinking about catching a body." There was even a Chaz look-alike contest going on.

Damn, I guess I am that bitch, Chaz said in her head, handing the girl back her phone. Then she spent the next thirty minutes entertaining the girls. So much so, it took for Dee-Dee to shut the shit down. Chaz tried to make the case that she didn't eat yet. However, Dee-Dee didn't care too much about her issues. She just wanted to leave.

Finally, after about two hours of catering to her fans in AppleBees the ladies left.

"Where to, my royalness?" jokingly asked Dee-Dee, as they got in the Buick.

"It doesn't even matter. Just get me the hell away from here." Chaz seemed a bit antsy.

Dee-Dee brought the engine to life and pulled out of the parking lot with no specific destination in mind. She just drove, enjoying the company of her woman without a care in the world. She stopped at the red light on Springfield Avenue and 10th Street. She began surfing the radio for a station of her liking. When the light turned green, Chaz took over the search.

"Girl, ain't shit on this radio. Pull into the gas station so I could buy one of those bootleg CD's," Chaz insisted.

Dee-Dee turned into the BP gas station. Chaz got out, and two minutes later she was back in the car with three CDs, two blunt wraps and a twenty sack of weed.

"I know you ain't get that weed from the guy behind the counter?" Dee-Dee asked with a half smirk.

Chaz looked at her like she had two heads.

"Now you know every gas station in Newark sell drugs. Shit, them Indians got coke, dope and smoke on standby," she said before popping in the latest Dave East mixtape.

The sun was in the process of receding as the ladies drove back to Jersey City. That's when Chaz got the bright idea of going to Liberty Park to smoke. She figured she'd get high before expressing her gratitude to Dee-Dee for all she's done. Because if it wasn't for Dee-Dee, Chaz would still be on the America's Most Wanted list.

It was about seven o'clock when they pulled into the park. "You wanna smoke in the car or over by the water," asked Chaz.

"I think it's best we don't smoke around here at all. We don't need no drama with the police. At least put some time between your last encounter and your next one. I mean you can't be too gangsta not to think."

Chaz thought about it. "Yeah, you right baby. Go to the house so we could enjoy ourselves to the fullest," she said seductively.

Chapter 5
Atlanta, Georgia

Detective Erica Sykes sat at her desk reviewing evidence from one of her rape cases. It was a case involving a forty-eight-year-old man and a little girl. It was a horrific case. What a shame, she thought as she screw-faced the photos of the victim. "How could you let this happen, God?" she questioned just as Mikros walked up.

"Hey there, you amazingly beautiful woman," he said excitedly.

Erica was relieved that someone pulled her attention away from the gut churning pictures she held in her hands. She tossed the photos on top of her desk and tried to plaster a smile on her face, but it wasn't working. The disgust was too evident. "Hey Mikros, what's up?" Her words were flat and hard.

He sensed that she was stressed. Unaware of himself, he placed four fingers over his mouth like he was making an Indian call. "Oh baby," he said in a worried woman's voice as he sat down. "What's wrong, what happened?" he asked grabbing Erica's hands.

"Oh, stop it," she pulled her hands back. "I'm just thinking about this case I've been working on."

"What case?"

"That aggravated rape and kidnapping case. The one with the guy from Harlem that got caught in the Adamsville section with that little girl in the abandoned house," Erica explained remorsefully.

"Oh yeah, the sick bastard from New York. Wow, that fucking guy is one hell of a whack job. But look here." Mikros smiled and smacked his lips. "As of today, you're not gonna have to deal with those unfortunate tragedies. You are officially re-assigned as my partner."

"Mikros, are you high?" She shot him a sideways stare.

"Only off life darling." He chuckled, then continued, "Now the Captain was gonna tell you himself, but I insisted that he let me break the news to you. At first, he tried to stick me with Detective Shaw. Girl, I was like oh hell no." Mikros started talking with his hands. "I said Captain, Shaw gotta bad heart, the last thing I need is for my partner to drop dead during an arrest! So, I insisted that he pull you out of special victims and partner us together," he expressed theatrically.

Erica couldn't do nothing but shake her head. She really thought Mikros was special, literally. She took a deep breath then relaxed. "Well, I'm flattered. 'Cause Lord knows special victims was busting my ass."

"Glad to see that you didn't object, 'cause in a few days we're going to New Jersey."

"Jersey? Why, what for?" she asked baffled.

"Give me a minute." Mikros shot over to his desk and hurried back. "Here," he said handing Erica a folder containing Adonis' file.

Nonchalantly, she opened the folder. "Damn! Is he a model or a criminal," she said louder than expected. She couldn't take her eyes off Adonis' mugshot. He looked like he was born to be in front of a camera. But it was unfortunate that the photographer of his head shot worked for the Department of Corrections. Unaware of herself, she began studying every detail of the heartthrob before her. From his golden-brown hair, to his dreamy hazel eyes, down to his chiseled jaw. I'd love to sit on this nigga's face, she thought.

"Uh, hello...," said Mikros waving his hand across the folder.

Erica looked up with a tight-lipped smirk. "What?" She laughed as the guilt of her thought lingered in the question.

"What my ass? He is fucking gorgeous," Mikros said adamantly..

She hissed, "Mikros you really need to see somebody." She closed the folder and put it on her desk.

"You're absolutely right, now give me back the file so I could see Mr. Davis again." He held his hand out in a serious attempt to get the folder back.

Erica stood up and put on her best—I'm sexy as hell so let me get my way face— "Well partner, I'm afraid I can't do that." She smiled vividly. "I have to get familiar with the case and I have limited time to do so." She snatched up the folder and clutched it tightly to her breast. "See ya tomorrow partner," she said giggling as she stepped off.

***

The minute Erica got into her car and pulled off, images from her previous rape case trampled through her mind. She just couldn't shake it. The utterly horrific ordeal that the victim suffered just continued to pound on her. "Ugh!" she growled as she strove to dismiss the thoughts of the images in her head.

Sykes pulled into her assigned parking spot at her apartment building and couldn't wait to get upstairs. She was gonna get justice for that little girl. And what she had in mind had nothing to do with the Criminal Justice System. She grabbed the files off the passenger seat and tossed them in her carrying case, then headed upstairs. Her strides were anxious and with attitude as she entered her building. "That nasty motherfucker needs his dick chopped off and shoved up his ass," she said while keying her way inside her apartment.

Once inside, she kicked her shoes off. "Uhm," she moaned in relief. Those heels had been tearing her feet up all day. After getting somewhat comfortable, she sat down in the living room and called her best friend Neesha. She knew if anybody could help her pull off some back door, illegal street justice, it was Neesha. The two had been best friends since second grade, and never allowed for the dynamics of their relationship to change. For over twenty years they served as each other's go to. It didn't matter what the situation was. Having a camaraderie like theirs was a rarity. They were so close one would have assumed they were fraternal twins. Same age-same career field, and oh yeah, they both had a thing for bad boys.

Neesha never answered her phone. After five rings it went to voicemail. "Neesha give me a call A.S.A.P. I gotta situation involving one of your tenants. Love you much." Erica marked the message urgent and hung up. Next, she decided to give Adonis' file a quick review. Time was winding down and she needed to get acquainted with the particulars of his case.

The sun was starting to set so she flicked on the table lamp. Followed by her diving into Adonis' rap sheet. Which ended up being a quick read. Because aside from two juvenile charges for assault, and the charges he was currently serving time for, his record was clean.

"Damn! I know them niggas in Jersey hate the judicial system," she stated after noticing the amount of time he was given for petty drugs and a gun. Then she started reading the details of the warrant.

"Fifteen!" she blurted out after reading that Adonis was only a teenager when he killed Travis. Her mind began racing a mile a minute. She started to unconsciously justify that there had to be some type of mix up. She just didn't wanna believe that a man so handsome was capable of murder.

Erica closed the folder and placed it on the table. Her eyes were getting heavy. Its been a long and mentally draining day. Getting some rest became her short-term goal. Ratchetly, she stretched out on the couch fully clothed, and fell asleep. And within an hour she was waking up. Not only was the couch uncomfortable, but her cell phone wouldn't stop ringing. Lethargically she sat up, pausing to collect herself. "Uhm, hello," she moaned into the TV remote. After taking notice of her mistake, she put the remote down and grabbed her phone. "Yeah," she answered, still sleepy.

"Why it take yo ass so long to answer the phone? Let me find out your lonely ass gotta nigga up there," Neesha said jokingly.

"Shit, I wish," Erica replied fully awoke at this point. "Yeah, but'um, I was calling you 'cause I gotta real live situation and—

"Say no more. I'm off Friday so I'll meet you for lunch and we'll talk then," Neesha chimed in. She knew whenever Erica make the reference 'real live situation' that it was serious.

"Well, how about next Friday 'cause I gotta go to Jersey in a few days and pick up a suspect," she replied as she walked to the bathroom to pee.

"A'ight, not a problem. Love you."

"Love you more," Erica replied ending the call. After relieving herself, she stripped down and jumped in the shower. The water temperature was just right, relaxing and soothing. As she lathered up, her mind began to wander. Quickly, she gained control of her thoughts. She didn't particularly like it when random shit popped in and out of her head. It made her feel weak.

She stepped back from under the water so she could watch the soap suds twirl down the drain. It was one of her childhood quirks that she seemed to still enjoy. Her eyes followed gleamingly while the suds swirled then disappeared. After the last of the suds had dissolved, she cut the water off and got out. Wet and stacked with beauty, she stood in front of the mirror and wrapped her hair in a towel. However, she didn't bother drying off. She elected to air dry. Then she brushed her teeth, flashed her gap tooth smile, and walked down to her bedroom. She looked at the clock on her nightstand. It was just past ten o'clock. There was a rumble in her stomach, as if noticing the time reminded her that she hadn't eaten. Quickly, she applied her deodorant, lotion and pussy spray then marched to the kitchen, still naked. Minutes later she was munching down on a plate of microwaved leftover beef and broccoli. By the time she was done eating, all she wanted to do was go to sleep. Chinese food for some reason always made her sleepy.

After cleaning up she made her way back to her room. As soon as she laid down another image of that god forsaken crime scene jumped back into her brain. "Fuck this," she spoke aloud. She climbed out of bed and retrieved her phone. "This shit can't wait, fuck that," she said as she dialed Neesha's number.

Neesha—aka Ms. Wallace—had just gotten off work and couldn't wait to get away from the jail. Even though she loved being a C.O., it was no secret that she dreaded being in that environment.

Erica's call came buzzing through as Neesha pulled off, heading home.

Neesha looked at her phone vibrating in the console and swiped the answer tab. "What's the problem, girl? You interrupting my glory moment," she expressed upon answering.

"You know damn well you ain't never glorious about nothing," Erica retorted.

"Don't be hating 'cause I gotta nigga at work that like to keep his face full of my farts," Neesha replied in reference to Pike.

"Girl, you nasty. Anyway, this shit can't wait till next Friday. Swing by my spot tonight. We gotta get a head start on this shit." The vastness of her demand screamed urgency.

"A'ight, I'm on my way. I'll be there in like twenty minutes." Neesha hung up. "I hope this bitch ain't stop taking her medication," she said as she continued to drive.

Chapter 6

South Woods State Prison

9:30 at Night

Qua laid in his bunk thinking about a bunch of nothing. When all of a sudden the sound of mail sliding under his cell door grabbed his attention. He jumped down to get it. Seeing that the letter was from Rep made him smile. Without delay he ripped the envelope open. Automatically, every feel good chemical in his brain began to go haywire. He couldn't believe his eyes.

"Rep you my nigga for real," he said while shuffling threw the pictures. Possessing those flicks really had him feeling like the king of convicts. And although there were no full front face shots, he could still tell that it was Chaz. Rep did a really good job of secretly taking those pics.

Qua held the photo's in is hands, transfixed on the delightful image of a real live gangsta bitch. And despite being cleared of all accusations, the media had already made her an icon in his eyes. In his mind, like so many others, Chaz wasn't anything less than a thoroughbred.

Qua climbed back in his bunk, still focused on the pictures. Stuck between shock and excitement, he couldn't wait to show her off. He flicked through them once more then put them under his mattress. About five minutes later he pulled them out and began obsessing over them. He was utterly awed that she was staying at his mother's house, and equally wowed that she was fucking with Dee-Dee. "Man, I gotta get mommy to bring this bitch up here for a visit," he said to himself out loud.

"Huh, what you say Qua?" his cellmate questioned from the bottom bunk.

Qua twisted his face up, "Nigga I ain't talking to ya nosy ass. Mind ya fucking business," he shot back.

For the remainder of the night Qua tortured himself with thoughts of freedom. All he could think about was the good ole days. The days when him and Rep would take turns fucking the chicks that worked for his mother. Then he wondered if Chaz was selling pussy. A feeling of elation cascaded through him. "Naw," he mumbled to himself. Before long, the sun was rising and shift was changing. He broke day without even realizing it. He was so caught up in his head that, if it wasn't for the loud mouth guard taking count, he would of lost sight of his reality. That's when he realized that it was the following day. He got up to take a piss and attend to his hygiene. Then out the clear blue, the thought of snatching his bunky out the bed and fucking him up flashed through his mind. Qua was impulsive like that. Luckily he chose to ignore the feeling.

It was a new day and he intended on showing his pictures off for the soul purpose of bragging rights. And of course, get props from Adonis. That was his main objective. Impressing Adonis was like a big deal for him. Kind of like a little boy seeking his big brother's approval.

Just as Qua finished grooming himself, count cleared. It was time for breakfast. When the door buzzed open he shot straight down to

Adonis' cell. "Yo my nigga, I got something to show you," he said smiling.

Adonis definitely wasn't in the mood to talk. It was early as hell and the last thing he expected was for Qua to show up at his cell on some joyous shit. "Damn nigga, you seem to be mighty fucking happy," he said in stride to the mess line as Qua walked alongside him.

"Yeah you know, regular shit," Qua stated kind of boastfully. Then with a smidge of composure he continued, "Here." He handed Adonis the pictures.

Adonis accepted the pictures and immediately began to feel different. His chest tightened and his heart pounded rapidly. He couldn't help it, his emotions got the best of him. Its been five years since he's seen his wife, Chantell. Also known to a selective few as his little sister. Nonetheless, Adonis was holding pictures of his other half, his only love, and his whole world. Frozen like a statue, he gaped intensely at the picture on top. A wide range of fluctuating feelings began to stir inside of him. He was slow to speak. He searched massively for the right words, any words, but nothing came out.

"Davis!" yelled the C.O. breaking Adonis' trance. "Keep it moving," he instructed.

Adonis handed Qua the pictures back with an artificial smile, "Damn, ain't that shorty that they just cleared of all those charges," he asked as he walked to grab his tray.

"Yeah that's her," Qua assured as he tucked the pictures back in his pocket and got his tray as well. The fellas entered the dining area and took a seat. Qua continued to mumble something, but Adonis had momentarily spaced out.

Although Adonis was physically functional, he sat at the table disconnected from reality. A blank expression captured his face as he picked through his food. There was no way possible for him to mask the feelings that ripped through him. Even though Qua had no knowledge that those pictures were of Adonis' wife, Adonis naturally felt betrayed.

Qua rose from the table to go show the pictures to a couple of his hometown homies. As expected, those fools damn near lost their minds. At first, jokers were bombing Qua. Saying that the pics were photoshopped. Just basically fucking with him. But Qua embraced it all in good humor, smiling as his boys busted on him.

Yet, Adonis didn't seem to find anything funny. It was killing him not to explode. Then suddenly, there was no more control. Adonis lost it. He jumped up and began throwing punches. The nigga he zeroed in on never seen it coming. Nor did anyone else for that matter.

Shock plagued the mess hall as Adonis released a six-punch combo, knocking the nigga out cold. Qua couldn't believe what just happened. Silence consumed the dining area as everyone gasped in surprise. Without speaking a word, Adonis stood tall and looked around with pure evilness captured in his eyes. He dared a motherfucker to say something. Thus, no one did. Then he walked out. Thankfully the C.O.'s weren't paying attention. Either that or they just didn't give a fuck.

Nobody understood why Adonis flipped out like that. But Qua wasn't naïve to the bullshit. He knew something was up. When he got back to his cell, he took himself back to the very first conversation him and Adonis had, in reference to Chaz. Then he said her name, "Chantell Davis." Baffled beyond belief, he held a closed fist up to his mouth. He was on to something, but wasn't exactly sure what that something was. He shot down to Adonis' cell. He needed to talk to him and get to the bottom of things. The last thing he wanted was for a wedge to be put between them. The two had grown to care for one another as if they were brothers, so if he felt that he was in violation, in any way, he had an obligation to rectify the situation.

Monk was exiting the cell as Qua approached. The two men head nodded to each other and continued with their business. Adonis stood at the back of his cell, gazing out the window.

Qua called out to get his attention. "Adonis."

When Adonis turned around, Qua could immediately tell that something was wrong. There was no way Adonis could mask his pain.

"Yo bro, we need to talk." Qua stepped inside the cell and posted up against the wall. The tenor of his voice clearly indicated concern.

"Naw man, we ain't got nothing to talk about," Adonis replied with his voice cracking.

"Yo son, you acting like a hoe. I don't know what the fuck is up with you, but you on some sensitive shit." Qua took the pictures out his pocket and sat them on the shelf. "Whoever she is to you, you could have told me. We been boys since day one. Truth be told, I never thought you'd be on it like that," he announced then walked out.

***

The second Qua entered his cell he snatched his bunky out the bed by his dreads and commenced to whooping his ass. This was one of his impulsive moments. The sound of hard thumping and muffled cries could be heard through the air vent. It was sad. But what was even sadder, was the fact that his bunky didn't even attempt to fight back. Meanwhile, Adonis had been called down to the Social Service Department to see Tonya Jackson. Going to see her couldn't have came at a better time. Having a sit down with her little sexy ass, was definitely gonna alleviate a lot of his stress. Not that Tonya's conversation could ever replace what him and Chaz shared, but it was good to have her around for a stress reliever. Especially given the fact that his current delima was what it was.

Adonis entered Tonya's office.

"Have a seat," she said nonchalantly.

He sat. "Yeah, what's up? Why you call me over here?"

"Don't flatter yourself. I got enough shit I'm dealing with. The last thing I need is for you to feel like I'm sweating you."

"Well clearly you got your own problems. Being married to that bitch ass nigga Moss is the biggest one!" he replied.

"Yeah, well, my issues ain't none of your concern. And I didn't call you over here for that." She rolled her eyes. "I called you over here to tell you that the Atlanta Police Department dropped a warrant on you. They'll be here to extradite you on the day you're released."

"Atlanta!?" He crossed his arms, "What the fuck are you talking about. Atlanta could kiss my ass. I ain't got no warrant down there. I haven't been to Atlanta in fifteen years." Then it hit him, "Oh shit!" he exclaimed. "Yo, what's the charge?"

"I don't know, but you don't have a bail," she explained.

Adonis didn't need her to tell him what the charge was, he had already figured it out. But what he couldn't seem to figure out was how in the world did the police find out about something that happened such a long time ago. He was baffled. "So basically, you telling me I gotta go handle this Atlanta shit before I get out." The devastating news showed greatly on his face.

Tonya's heart sank, she felt awful that she had to be the one to tell him. "Listen Adonis, I wasn't supposed to tell you this. But I told you because I love you and I really wanna see you get out of this hellhole. So never mind all the bullshit, tell me what you need me to do and it's done." The sincerity in her words spoke volumes.

Trapped in deep disbelief, he blankly stared ahead. Then he spoke, "Yeah, as a matter of fact there is something I need you to do." He grabbed a piece of paper and pen off her desk and wrote a quick note. "Here. Take a few days off and handle this for me. I need you to help me get up out this mess." He was dictating with authority. "I got a little less than two days before Atlanta come to get me, so I need to be ready."

Tonya glanced down at what he wrote and brought her eyes back up to meet his. "Are you sure you want me to follow this?" she asked unsurely.

He looked at her with extreme sternness and leaned forward,

"Absolutely!" he growled.

When he got back to his unit, his main focus was to find Qua. He needed to not only clear the air with the man he'd grown to love as a brother, but he also needed to enlist Qua's help in a number of ways. Because as sure as a pig's pussy is pork, shit had just got real. Adonis shot to the dayroom area where there was a poker game in progress. Of course, Qua was dead smack in the middle of it. Adonis entered the recreation room and instantly his presence promoted a few scary niggas to feel uneasy.

Nonetheless, Qua was at the table talking cash shit, knocking jokers off their game. "Anything less than a flush is a bust and two pair can't win. Sorry fellas, but this full house gonna put me all in."

Adonis cracked a light smile as Qua arrogantly reached for the winnings. "Yo, Mr. Card Shark, let me holla at you real quick," he said grinning.

Qua didn't even wait for the question to settle. He was up from the table in a flash. "I'm cashing out," he said. "I got something to do. I'll see y'all sweet knuckle niggas later."

Adonis just shook his head laughing. Qua was a real character at times.

"What up tho?" he asked as he approached Adonis. Qua was the type of dude that didn't harbor feelings when it came to petty shit. In his mind, he had no issue with Adonis. He still looked at the man in the same light as always. Not to mention, he took his stress on his bunky earlier.

"Nothing much, I just wanted to holla at you about a few things that's all," answered Adonis.

"Man knock it the fuck off, you my bro. That shit from earlier wasn't 'bout nothing. Plus my bunky already paid for your sins. I whooped that nigga ass in the name of Jesus."

"Nigga you crazy. I'ma holla at you later on in the yard. I got some things to share with you."

"A'ight, say less."

Chapter 7

At the same time, down in Maryland: A trucker pulled into a rest area. He had been on the road all night and desperately needed a break. He could barely keep his eyes open. It was about three o'clock Wednesday afternoon and he figured he'd catch a nap until nightfall, then hit the road again. He parked his rig and got out.

"Come on now girl, go stretch ya legs," he commanded his K-9.

Bella jumped out the truck wagging her tail with excitement. She sprung back and forth leaping into the air. "Ruff, Ruff," Bella barked.

"A'ight now, gone run around for a bit. We's ain't gonna be long," commanded the scruffy thin framed trucker.

The trucker walked towards the restrooms as his dog ran about aimlessly. He walked into the restroom and winced at the smell of urine musk lingering in the air. Smells awful, he thought in the process of relieving himself. Just when he began to drain his bladder the aggressive barks and growls from his K-9 could be heard filling the air. "What in the world is that dog out there doing?" he questioned himself. When he got back outside, the dog was committed to an uncharacterized stance over by the dumpster. That crazy dog wouldn't let up, she just continued to bark viciously at the dumpster.

"What, what is it girl?" he asked as if the dog could explain that she smelled the decayed human remains inside the dumpster. Nonetheless, the guy must have gone nose blind from the stench in the restroom, because he couldn't smell anything outside of garbage and dumpster juice. The guy looked around as if something unusual would immediately jump out at him. But there wasn't anything. Still, his dog carried on, barking thunderously.

The guy approached the dumpster cautiously, then reluctantly he opened the top. BOOM! He jumped when the flap smacked against the back of the trash container. Instantly, he knew why his dog had been throwing a tantrum. The intense malodorous smell that rose from that dumpster caused him to vomit immediately. He threw up everything except his stomach. The man stumbled back a few feet, then dropped to one knee. Bile spewed from his mouth like running water. It seemed like it took him an eternity to collect himself. Then about a minute or so later, made it back over to the dumpster. At this point, he wanted to see what was in there more so out of curiosity than concern. He covered his mouth and nose as he approached the dumpster. "Oh god!" he yelled inside his hand then turned away. Again, he began to gag and vomit. After going through the motions, he scurried back to his rig, using his CB radio to call in what he had just discovered. "Breaker breaker, this— then suddenly he stopped when he saw a Maryland State Police car running idle. He dropped the receiver and made a dash to the police car.

"Officer! Officer!" he yelled out, flailing his arms in the air.

"What the hell does this fool want?" The officer questioned himself, sitting his coffee cup in its holder. The officer exited the car just as the man approached. "Sir, sir," he gasped. "There's human remains over in the dumpster. Human remains!" the trucker shouted dramatically.

"Slow down their fella. Just what'n the devil is you yapping about?" asked the officer with a confused look on his face.

The trucker took a deep breath. "Sir, there's rats and maggots over in the dumpster feasting on human remains," he described in shock.

The officer took a moment to study the man's face. "Boy are you high?" he demanded to know while placing his hand on his service pistol.

"No sir, I ain't high and I'm not crazy." He got real theatrical. "Now like I said, there's a dead body over there being eaten by a group of rats and maggots."

The officer never took his hand off his Glock as he turned in the direction of where the man was pointing to. "A'ight then, gone and lead the way. Show me what you're talking about."

The man led the way while his dog could still be heard barking up a storm. "You hear that, that's my bitch carrying on like that. She's the one that discovered that nasty shit," he spat in a light country drool.

Cautiously, the officer stepped to get close to the origin of the foul odor. Immediately his stomach bubbled, flipped and churned as the smell invaded his nostrils. "Jesus Christ!" he shouted, putting his hand over his nose. Finally, he got close enough to look inside. And sure as a crab ass is waterproof, there were thousands of maggots getting fat off Patty-Mae and Teesha's decomposed heads. "Ugh!" the officer winced in disgust.

"I told ya. I fucking told ya," bellowed the man excitedly.

"Look, take your dog and go wait by my cruiser. This here's a crime scene now and you're a witness. So—

"Whoa! Wait one minute," he screamed cutting the officer short. "The last thing I got time for is answering a bunch of questions. I gotta get—

"You gotta get your ass over there by my cruiser and wait till I get

there, or I'ma lock you and that barking bitch up. Now gone, get!"
yelled the officer just before calling in the situation over his radio.

The man called his dog and strolled off mumbling to himself. He
was mad that he let his curiosity get the best of him. All he wanted
to do was take a piss and catch a nap. But from the looks of things
he had gotten himself in a world of shit. For a moment, he thought
about hopping in his rig and skating off, but quickly dismissed the
thought when he heard the sirens getting closer.

Within minutes, there were several more Maryland State Police
cars pulling into the rest area.

The officer that called it in stood center mass in the parking
lot, directing colleagues over to where the maggot feast—hosted
by Patty-Mae and Teesha's severed heads—was being held. Light
screeches blessed the pavement as the cars came to a complete stop.

"What is it Johnny?" asked the first trooper that got out of his car.

"The dumpster!" The trooper pointed with a horrified look on his
face.

Chapter 8

Wednesday night,

Fulton County Jail

Flex was attempting to call his mother when he noticed a new inmate walking towards his cell. He hung up. "Yo, I hope you don't think you going in cell eight?" he stated as he approached the guy. It was no way in hell he was about to be cell mates with a crackhead. Especially a crackhead who was fucked up from the feet up. The man could barely stand up straight. And he looked to have a rug glued to his head. But that was no rug, just an extreme case of nigga naps and neglect.

The rail thin fiend collected enough heart to look Flex square in the eyes and say, "Nigga, I think it's best you fuck with me some other time. I ain't in the mood for no bullshit."

No one on the tier expected the fiend to snap on Flex like that. Then out of nowhere, New York put the shit talking crackhead on his ass. Wham! New York hit the man with a monstrous right hand.

It was obvious that he was trying to score points with Flex. The C.O.'s looked on from their booth but never attempted to move.

New York dragged the guy by his ankles over by the officer station. He looked in the booth then shouted, "This nigga gotta go!"

Flex watched on silently. Thinking to himself that New York just might be the flunky he needed to put himself in a better position. Flex went back over to the phone to call his mother. He dialed the number and waited anxiously for her to accept his call. His heart skipped a beat when he heard the sweet tone of her voice.

"Hello," she answered.

"Yeah ma, it's me," he replied quite humbly.

His mother hadn't heard his voice in what seemed like ages. The last time she did, he sounded nothing like the man she birthed. "Oh Michael," she stated compassionately. "Are you alright in there? Is everything alright?" she asked. Her questions was more out of motherly concern than out of fear that he couldn't handle himself.

"Yeah ma, I'm good. But I really need to see you." Just after he spoke, he heard the cries of a small child in the background."

"James, put that down!" Sharon shouted away from the receiver. I'm listening Michael."

He paused as the name James registered in his mind. Instantly, he thought back to Mack. Followed by Tay's face popping into his head. "Ma who you talking to?" Flex questioned.

"Oh, that's little James. I've had him for quite some time now. One night Norris had come by and asked me to watch him, but he never came back." The pain Sharon felt following the last part of her statement took her to another place emotionally.

Flex could hear the hurt in his mother's voice. Very briefly he felt a little guilty. He knew how much his mother loved the late Norris Kliens. "Listen Ma, I really need for you to come visit me this weekend. I can't talk to you over the phone, but make sure you get up here."

"I'll be there Michael, don't worry. Now do you need anything, money or anything at all?"

"Actually, I do. Put about two hundred in my account."

"Okay I'll do that in the morning," she replied. Reminding him of the confident, trustworthy mother he had known in his early childhood.

Flex smiled internally. It felt wonderful to have his mother back. "A'ight ma, I'ma call you tomorrow night. I love you."

"I love you too, Michael."

Flex hung up the phone feeling at ease. At least for the moment. That phone call to his mother momentarily pulled him away from the harsh realities of his circumstances. He was confident that things weren't as bad as they seemed. But his confidence and the facts of the matter didn't coincide. Truth be told, he was fucked.

New York approached, "Yo son. I'ma holla at you next day!" he said while extending his fist for a dap.

"Word, next day," responded Flex while obliging the gesture. When he got in his cell the first thing he did was drop to his knees and began praying. It was something about that phone call that promoted him to call on the Lord. Its been years since he had a talk with God. Even though his fate was damn near sealed. Thanking God for giving him back his mother was more than a reason to be grateful.

Meanwhile, Pike and Neesha Wallace were having themselves a good ole time in a secluded part of the jail. After having that talk with Erica a few nights ago, Neesha was convinced that she needed to be a little— shall we say— nicer to Pike, if she was gonna enlist his help to get justice for Erica's rape victim. Because with the respect and pull that Pike had around the jail, giving him some pussy would sure as shit get the job done.

"You know I been thinking about letting yo lil young ass eat my pussy." Neesha smiled then continued, "You got those LL lips. I bet you wouldn't mind tasting this rainbow," she giggled.

Pike began blushing like a schoolgirl. "Ms. Wallace you crazy. You know I'm sweet on you, right? Don't be getting me all amped up like you gone let me knock dem walls down." He smiled gripping himself.

Her eyes followed his hand movement. "Uhm!" she moaned, licking her lips seductively. "Let me see that dick?" she said working her eyes.

Totally caught off guard, Pike blushed. Though he had nothing to be shy about. Without blinking he exposed himself. "Girl you can't call me out like that. I'm really 'bout that, ya hear me." His country twang peeked as he spoke those words confidently. Swoosh! He dropped his pants.

At first sight Neesha couldn't help but feel a little intimidated by the size of his shaft. She hadn't expected for his young ass to be packing meat like a slaughterhouse. "Are you sure that thing is normal?" she asked in all seriousness.

His dick hung long and thick with massive veins popping out. It had to be at least eight inches while soft. "Never mind all that, you wanted to see it so I'm showing you. But to answer your question, yeah. It's normal for me. Shit, it's the only gift my no-good daddy ever gave me," he chuckled.

Neesha didn't really find what Pike said to be funny. "Well, we ain't doing nothing anyway. You ain't 'bout to bust my pussy open with that monster. Put it away." she said feeling a bit uncomfortable.

Respectfully, he tucked his junk away. "See, you act like you with it, but you just a tease," he told her.

"Pike you can't be serious. The last thing I am is a tease." Her face embodied a disgruntled look. "You could say what you want. But if it don't fit don't force it. Now here's the deal, either you eat my pussy and I try to suck that gigantic thing yo daddy gave you. Or we could just call it a night. I got about fifteen minutes to get you back to your unit before count," she informed him while looking at her watch.

"Oh you serious, huh? Shit! Come on den, let a nigga get his grub on!"

Neesha cracked a tight-lipped smile as she wiggled down her uniform pants. She couldn't believe what she was about to do. Finally, she was gonna break her moral virginity and let Pike suck on her sweetness.

He stood there watching in a daze as she prepped to serve him his last meal of the night. He was anxious as hell to get some type of sexual gratification.

"Lay down so I could sit on your face," she stated with a seductive giggle.

With the quickness he got down on the floor. Then suddenly they heard the jingle of keys approaching the supply closet.

"Oh shit!" she screamed in a whisper as she rushed to collect herself.

Pike scrambled up off the floor. He was nervous as hell. Instantly his dick deflated and his heart pounded rapidly. And just in the nick of time, a fellow correction officer opened the closet door only to find Pike stacking cleaning supplies while Neesha checked the items off on her clipboard.

"Hey Wallace, you got about five minutes before count time. So hurry up. I don't want any trustees on my count," stated the slim, goofy looking white C.O.

Neesha flashed a—kiss my ass nigga—look his way. "Uhn hmm, I got you."

***

When Pike got back to his dorm he laid in his bunk obsessing over the situation with Ms. Wallace. Almost to the point of driving himself crazy. The image of her stout legs and cleanly shaved pussy became a permanent fixture in his mind. A fixture so vivid he could smell the sweet tartness of her womb as if it was present in his face. "Fuck!" he exclaimed inside his head as he adjusted his hard on. "Man fuck this," he mumbled to himself before grabbing the Vaseline and a ButtMan magazine out of his locker. Then headed straight to the bathroom. And yeah, well you know the rest.

***

After Neesha Wallace got off work she called Erica. They needed to discuss a few things. Particularly the close encounter Neesha had with getting caught. "Hey girl," she said when Erica answered.

"Nothing much, just watching Love & Hip-Hop. Girl, these reality shows are off the hook. I'm telling you, we could do that shit way better than them busted ass bitches."

"I know that's right, and speaking of busted. Bitch I'm on my way over to your house as we speak. I got some reality shit for that ass," Neesha told her with a ghetto overtone.

"A'ight. I'ma be outside waiting on you."

"Well hurry up cause I'm right round da conna," Neesha replied.

"A'ight." Erica hung up and got out the bed. She slipped on her slippers and robe, then strutted her thick, pretty ass down stairs. At that exact moment Neesha was pulling up.

"Get in the car, I ain't staying long," Neesha said out the window as she parked.

Erica got in, "Okay, so what the fuck happened?" she asked hastily in the process of shutting the car door.

"Damn, you saying it like you my pimp or something," Neesha retorted with disdain.

Erica gave her a sideways look. "Bitch knock it off. Just tell me what happen cause I gotta get some sleep. I gotta busy day tomorrow."

"Well first of all, I'm not giving Pike no pussy. That nigga's dick 'bout long as my arm and fat as my leg. Girl I think he got something. I ain't never seen a nigga with a dick that big in real life."

Erica's face lit up with confusion. She had never known Neesha to be intimidated of a big dick.

"What you mean you think he got something? It's called a big dick, duh!"

"No bitch, that shit ain't normal. He holding like he was genetically engineered in a lab or something. That shit ain't normal." Neesha

47

spoke as if she was angry.

"A'ight then, so that's it? That's all you had to tell me?"

Neesha jerked her head back, "Ill, bitch you bugging. You really think you some type of Madam, huh?"

Erica sighed as she tried to maintain her composure, "Look Neesha, all things serious, are you gonna help me or not. You seen those pictures of that little girl. I gotta get that nigga Tyrone. Now if you can't help me out 'cause you all of a sudden scared of a Mandingo, then you need to let me know. But regardless of what, that nigga Tyrone sick ass gonna pay for what he did." Erica's emotional spew put Neesha in a different place. A place that all females could draw from when needing a reason to do a nigga some harm.

"Yeah E, I got you. But just for the record, I ain't about to fuck my insides up tryna to get justice for your victim. Because I'm telling you, that nigga's dick ain't human."

Chapter 9

Thursday morning,

Bridgeton, NJ

Tonya woke up at her usual time, despite only getting three hours of sleep. She had been up most of the night thinking about many things. Her thoughts ranged from the fetus inside her to the instructions Adonis had given her to follow. She was absolutely driving herself crazy. How in the world could she walk away from Adonis at this point, knowing his situation. But not for nothing, she loved that man. She loved him with a strange obligation that would often override her common sense.

Tonya looked over at her husband in disgust. Instantly, she was motivated to do what Adonis had asked of her. She got up out the bed, grimacing at her snoring husband. Regret for marrying such an anal sphincter gripped her. Nasty bastard, she thought as she walked towards the bedroom door. On cue, Moss let out a thunderous fart.

Tonya looked back. "Ugh," she said then made her way to the bathroom.

And not even ten seconds had passed before Moss came waltzing his funky ass in behind her. "Damn, don't you see me in here," she stated distastefully.

Moss attempted to say something but stopped himself. He walked off with an attitude. Immediately, Tonya locked the door behind him. She hated when he interrupted her. She cut the water on in the sink while catching a glimpse of herself in the mirror. It was something about the way her reflection stared back at her that gave her a spark. She smiled as she rubbed her stomach. Little Adonis, she thought. It was that elated thought that promoted her to wanna carry on with helping Adonis any way she could.

When she opened the bathroom door Moss was standing there in the hallway. She acted as if his presence didn't bother her, but it did. She didn't need for him to start up with his bullshit.

"So, you wanna tell me why you took the day off?" he asked suspiciously.

Her skin began to crawl. She felt uneasy and a bit nervous. Her eyes shifted unconsciously. "Ahhh," she stuttered. Then there was a drastic change in her demeanor. She went from timid to terror. "None of your fucking business. And who the hell do you think you are keeping tabs on me. Fuck outta here!" she snapped, pushing past him.

"But baby," he whined while following behind her.

"But my ass," she stopped just inside their bedroom. She turned to face him with a look of hatred in her eyes. "When are you gonna get the picture, huh?" She began counting off with her fingers. "I haven't fucked you in God knows how long. I barely talk to you. The only reason we still living together is cause I'm saving money to move out. Don't you get it, I don't love you anymore. Its been that way for quite some time now." She turned and walked into the bedroom.

"But baby," he called out as she retrieved her powder blue Jumpman tracksuit from the closet. "What's the problem, where did we go wrong?" he inquired in a super sensitive tone.

The complexion of his question irked her nerves. She hated a weak ass man. Moss may have been a tough guy at work, but outside of that he was a hoe ass nigga.

Tonya never responded. She had things to do. Things that were far more important than what he was crying about.

After about a full minute of standing there looking stupid, Moss carried his attitude down to the living room. He couldn't stand when she acted like that. It made him feel weak. As if he didn't measure up as a man. Nonetheless that was something he was dealing with. Tonya could have cared less.

It was around seven o'clock by the time Tonya had finished getting dressed. She wasn't trying to do too much. She kept it simple: track suit, matching Jordans, and of course a North Carolina fitted hat. She checked her purse for the note Adonis had written, grabbed her car keys and proceeded to get on her way.

Moss got up off the couch to peek through the blinds. He was clocking her every move. "Bitch must think I'm stupid," he said out loud to himself as she got in her car and pulled off.

Tonya stopped off at the local Seven Eleven to get a cup of coffee and a bagel. She had to drive a good distance. So putting something in her stomach was a must. Anyway, when she pulled into the parking lot she could have sworn she saw Adonis. She had to do a double take. Then she realized it was the guy that worked there. "This nigga really got my mind spun," she spoke out loud as she got out to go inside.

Within minutes, she was back in her black Audi A4 headed towards the highway. She was on a mission. A mission to help Adonis get home. She found a nice R&B satellite station and drove her little tail off. Weaving in and out of traffic with pleasurable thoughts of the man that put a smile on her face and joy in her heart.

***

Meanwhile at Rep's apartment

Rep rolled off of Monique with sweat dripping from his brow. He had given that ass a good pounding for all of twenty minutes. It was customary for him to slide up in her every morning. He became accustomed to getting up in her wholesome goodness right after his early morning piss. It was just something about fucking Monique to get his day started that gave him reason to feel like that nigga.

"Uhm, you a beast," Monique moaned with her legs still arched as Rep's nut oozed from her slit.

He laid next to her breathing hard. "Well..." he paused then continued while trying to catch his breath, "I guess the beautiful feeling of your insides would make us the modern-day Beauty and the Beast," he chuckled.

"Ahh. See baby, when you say shit like that it be having me feeling like you really do love me. Even though you don't wanna actually admit it." She turned to face him.

"I don't give a fuck what you think. I don't love you, and you need to stop believing that shit." He sat up. "Now go cut the shower on and heat me up some Pop-Tarts," he instructed.

"I swear you get on my nerves. I'ma stop giving you this bomb ass pussy, that'll make yo ass confess that you love me, even if it's only to get a nut."

He busted out laughing. "Bitch, you crazy. That ain't gonna make me confess shit. What's gonna happen is, I'ma end up putting yo ass out my apartment. I'd love to do that," he spat with venomous sarcasm.

Monique sucked her teeth and rolled her eyes. "What is your problem? Why the fuck you always gotta be like that!" She got up and stormed out the room.

"Cause I gotta mean fuck game and I pay the bills 'round this motherfucker, that's why!" he yelled. Ending his spiel with his best Jadakiss impersonation, "Ah ha."

Monique didn't have the energy to argue. Jumping in the shower before the hot water pressure dropped was her objective. Just as she stepped under the showerhead, Rep walked in to join her. She gave him an awkward glance without saying a word. He peeped her attitude and found it to be funny, though he never laughed.

He lathered his wash rag and handed it to her, "Here scrub my back."

Monique snatched the washcloth out his hand. "I can't stand yo ass," she pouted.

Rep turned around so she could wash his back. He struggled not to laugh. He found it amusing that she bore tantrums the way she did. But little did he know, she was smiling as well. Suddenly, she wedged her soapy hand deep between his ass cheeks. "Ohh!" he screamed as his eyes nearly jumped out his head. He spun around with the quickness. Instinctively, he hit her with a swift left uppercut followed by a right over hand. Boom-Bam, was the sound that echoed off her face as she fell, landing awkwardly.

"Bitch! You must be out yo rabbit ass mind. I ain't with that Battiboy shit!" he bellowed in anger.

She was out cold. But oh well, he didn't give a fuck. In his mind the bitch shouldn't have violated.

Rep shut the water off and carried her into the bedroom. Naked and wet, he laid her down on the bed and proceeded to get dressed. Just like that, his concern for her at that moment was none existent. He had shit to do, and attending to her silly ass wasn't on his agenda. After getting himself straight he left to go meet up with Chaz and Dee-Dee. The three of them had made plans to hang out and enjoy themselves to the fullest.

It was about 9:45 in the morning when he pulled up in front of the house on Ocean Avenue. He had just parked his Jeep when his phone went off. "Hello," he answered, grabbing the half blunt out the ashtray.

"You have a collect call from—Qua." Rep accepted the call and put the phone on speaker as he lit his blunt. "Yeah, what up bro," said Rep sparking his blunt.

"Ah yo, I need you to bust a move for me A.S.A.P. like yesterday," Qua expressed anxiously.

Rep took a deep tote of the Kush, "Damn nigga, ain't you mighty eager to get some shit done," he said exhaling.

"Naw, peep game. I need you to go by my mom's house and put Dee-Dee on the phone. It's mad important my nigga!"

"Well you called at the right time 'cause I'm sitting outside your mom's crib as we speak. Hold on, I'm 'bout ta go and get her right now."

Qua covered the receiver and looked at Adonis who was standing right next to him. "He 'bout to put Dee-Dee on the jack right now."

"Dee-Dee!" yelled Rep as he entered the house.

"I'm in the kitchen," she responded.

Rep entered the kitchen. "Here, Qua wanna holla at you," he said handing Dee-Dee the phone.

"Hey Quaheem, what's going on?" she asked.

"Yeah, I'm good. Now peep game. Your girlfriend's brother is down here with me and he really need to speak to her. So do me a favor and put her on the phone," Qua explained.

"A'ight, but don't he get out tomorrow? We were coming down there to pick him up," she said while heading upstairs to give Chaz the phone.

"That's why he gotta talk to her. Oh yeah, when the hell is my mother coming back?" he questioned.

Hearing him inquire about Patty-Mae left her with a lump the size of a peach in her throat. Guilt probed at her. "Uh uhm, huh? Oh, here you go Chaz." Dee-Dee handed her the phone. She made it her business to avoid Qua's question.

Chaz looked at her befuddled, "Who is it?" she asked as she accepted the phone.

"Your brother."

"What, my brother?" she questioned before sitting up on the bed. "Hello," Chaz said more like a question than a greeting.

Mr. Ish

"Hold on," Qua responded then handed Adonis the phone.

"Hey baby girl, what's going on?" Adonis stated calmly. The texture of his voice sent a blistering chill of excitement down Chaz's spine.

"Oh my God," she whispered back as tears of joy invaded her face. "Adonis," she called out in a crackling tone. She couldn't believe it. Its been forever and a day since she heard his voice.

"Listen Chaz, I'm not coming home tomorrow. Atlanta is coming to get me 'cause I have a warrant down there. But don't you worry about none of that. I'ma figure this out, believe that. I got somebody coming to see you and they'll explain things a little more in detail. She'll do whatever you need her to do. Understand?"

Chaz was stumped. She felt disconnected and once again abandoned. "No Adonis, I need you home tomorrow." She began crying a river. She couldn't go on without having him in her life. She had been through too much and had suffered too many heartbreaks and let downs for this to be happening. "Please tell me you're joking, please Adonis. I need you home," she boohooed.

Adonis felt as though he had failed her in so many ways. All of the promises he made to love and protect her had come back to discredit him. He had to figure it out, he just had to. "I love you Chaz. Believe me, we'll get through this," he stated with genuine sincerity. Then the phone clicked off.

Chaz sat on the bed in a daze. Dee-Dee could see the pain in her face, it was evident. "What's wrong Chaz? What happened?" Dee-Dee questioned, sitting down next to Chaz on the bed. And before Chaz could respond, Rep yelled upstairs.

"Dee-Dee, some lady named Tonya is at the door for Chaz!"

Chapter 10

Thursday afternoon,

South Woods State Prison

Lunch had just been terminated and Adonis hadn't left his cell since talking to Chaz a few hours ago. He wasn't in the mood for socializing. His mind was wrapped around being transferred to Atlanta. He couldn't even enjoy the fact that he heard the sweet, tender voice of his beautiful wife. Then out of nowhere, Mustaheem's face popped into his head. Anger filled him. Faggot ass nigga, he thought.

Although Adonis wanted to blame Mu for the circumstances of his predicament, he could only place the blame on himself. He was just now starting to understand where he went wrong. And that learning experience would be one for the books.

Monk entered the cell just as Adonis pushed the image of Mu out of his head. It was obvious that something troubling was on Monk's mind. His disgruntled look said it all.

"Man, I'm tired of these motherfuckers 'round here," Monk exclaimed with hatred in his voice.

"What happen my nig?" Adonis asked.

Monk didn't respond, he just stood over the sink huffing and puffing at his reflection. Adonis didn't probe any further. Then Monk finally spoke, "That bitch ass nigga lieutenant Moss came down to the kitchen and started questioning me about you."

Adonis' antennas went up. Monk had his full attention at this point. "Me? Why would he be asking about me?" he inquired with weariness. Playing it off as if he didn't know. Which was the correct response, giving the fact that he never told Monk about him Tonya. Not that Monk had loose lips, but Adonis just didn't move like that.

"Man fuck that fat, clown ass nigga. I ain't sweating that shit. He just another miserable motherfucker tryna bring a brother down."

"Yeah, I hear you. But I still wanna know what him being miserable got to do with me?" Adonis questioned.

Monk started laughing, "Yo, that's one insecure dude. Either that or he just envious of you. That nigga asked me if you ever mentioned having a thing for Mrs. Jackson."

"Mrs. Jackson?" Adonis said acting as if he had the slightest clue about what Monk was talking about.

"Yeah, the social worker bitch with the fat ass," explained Monk.

"Nigga I know who she is. Man, that dude tripping. I ain't thinking about no bitch at a time like this. Shit, the way these crackers playing, I might not be focused on bitches for a long time."

"Well as long as you ain't converting from broads to bros, we good," Monk said laughing.

"Fuck outta here!" And no sooner than Adonis said that their cell door popped open.

Low and behold, stood Lieutenant Moss with a few of his henchmen. "Davis, step out," stated Moss with a destructive look in his eyes.

Adonis didn't hesitate in the least. He stepped out of that cell fitted in arrogance. His lack of respect for Moss showed that he wasn't pressed for the bullshit. Atlanta would be there in the morning to extradite him, and that's all he was focused on.

"Go sit up front," instructed Moss with a dirty look.

Adonis could feel the soul piercing stares from the accompanying C.O.'s. He just knew they hated his ass. "Not a problem sir," Adonis replied sarcastically as he walked off. When he got up front, the unit officer told him to wait in the TV room. As soon as he got inside the C.O. locked him in. Adonis clicked on the television. His ego smiled. He found it amusing that Moss was running around acting like a hoe. "I see why your wife gave me the pussy," he said to himself as he sat down. Then there was a blaring code 33 resonating loudly over the PA system. Adonis jumped up and ran to the window, watching on as the response team filed onto his unit. "Fuck!" Adonis screamed after realizing what Moss was really up to. This was something he didn't see coming. He wasn't expecting this by no means.

Initially, Adonis thought Moss and his goons were there to trash his cell. But that wasn't the case at all. Moss knew that he had to turn Adonis over to the state of Georgia in good health. So, Moss decided to take his beef—with Adonis—out on Monk. It was count time and everybody was locked in. Such the perfect time for Moss to get his shit off.

Adonis gawked through the window of the TV room. Guilt and rage consumed him. All he could do was hope and pray that Monk fucked one of them up as well. Even though he knew Monk was a thoroughbred and could hold his own. He also knew that the odds were stacked against him. That was a straight bitch move, Adonis thought as he waited impatiently for any signs of Monk. About thirty seconds later Monk was being dragged out.

"You faggot ass nigga!" shouted Adonis while banging on the window. The sight of Monk's limp body being dragged out like a piece of trash infuriated him. "Y'all some bitches! Come in here and try that shit on me! Come on you bitch ass niggas!" he screamed then started kicking on the door. All types of pinned up stress and aggravation began to surface as his tantrum kicked into high gear. "I'd fuck all y'all up, all y'all!" he continued to yell out angrily.

Moss walked over to the TV room window and instructed for his henchmen to hold Monk's head up. He wanted Adonis to get a good look at the damage his calvary caused. And boy did they cause some damage.

Monk was out cold and so was a few of his teeth and dreads. His eyes were swollen shut and blood spewed from his face like water from a faucet.

Immediately tears fell from Adonis' eyes. His heart sank, there was no way to describe the pain he felt for his comrade.

A shitty grin spread the length of Moss' face. He took pride in making sure Adonis felt the effects of his wrath. "Don't worry Mr. Davis, we'll take good care of your friend. Enjoy your trip to Atlanta," Moss said as he walked away from the window.

Adonis had no words. He was mad beyond the norm, but there was nothing he could do at the moment. Though at first chance, he was gonna make sure he made Moss suffer in the worst way.

***

Meanwhile
Down in Atlanta

Detective Erica Sykes and Mikros were boarding their flight that was scheduled to leave for Philadelphia. Initially, they were going to drive to New Jersey and get Adonis, but it was just so much easier to catch a plane to Philadelphia then drive to South Woods, being as though the prison was only an hour from Philly's airport.

"Girl, are you serious? You mean to tell me that you ain't never thought about fucking any of the guys you arrested," Mikros asked Erica in a whisper as they took their seats.

"Mikros you crazy. Only you could come up with something like that," she replied.

"Yeah, but you still ain't answer my question," he said smiling.

"Well I don't think that's a question worth answering." The tone of her response said it all.

"I respect that. But I gotta be honest, there's just too many sexy thugs out there for me not to think about one of them running up in my tight, white asshole."

"Mikros!" Erica shouted louder than she expected. A few passengers looked at her like she was a typical hood-rat with no home training. She was so embarrassed.

Mikros put his head down, snickering at her expense.

She was heated. "Mikros, I really hope you don't act a fool when we get to the prison. 'Cause I ain't got time for your nonsense." As soon as Erica finished talking the flight attendant announced that the flight was gonna be delayed for at least two hours, due to mechanical issues.

"You know this is some bullshit, right? It seems like mother justice always throwing a monkey wrench into the equation. Lord knows I'm anxious to see that tall handsome suspect of ours." Mikros just couldn't stop, he was all the way turnt up.

Erica rolled her eyes at his ratchet comment. She was now starting to understand why no one wanted to be his partner. It had nothing to do with his sexual preference, but everything to do with the way he conducted himself. Erica excused herself and went to the restroom. More so to get away from Mikros than for any other reason. Once inside she took a seat and pulled out her phone to call Neesha.

"Hey girl, I was just about to call you," Neesha reported after answering.

"Yeah, I bet you was. Let me guess, Pike's dick done grew an extra six inches and now you definitely can't help a bitch out," Erica said laughing.

"Ha ha very funny, you should of been a comedian. Anyway, I was about to call and tell you that Pike got released about an hour ago. He went to court and they gave him probation."

Mr. Ish

Erica was saddened. All she could see was red and all she could feel was pain. "Well I guess I'ma have to wait for the courts to deal with that sick ass nigga, Tyrone. Fuck!" She shouted in frustration. She was really banking on Neesha's help. "A'ight then, let me get off this phone. I'ma holla at you later."

"Okay girl, I'll talk to you later." Neesha hung up and looked over at Pike, "You ready baby?" she asked as she pulled off with her new boo riding shotgun.

When Erica got back to her seat the thought of requesting to sit somewhere else crossed her mind. Being next to Mikros just added even more disgust to the way she was feeling.

"So, you mean to tell me that you wouldn't give this gorgeous ass gangsta no pussy," Mikros whispered as he held Adonis' mugshot in his hand.

Despite being angry as hell, Erica couldn't deny the pussy pulsating features of Adonis. Nonetheless, she was too pissed and disappointed to lust over a man. Especially a man that was about to be extradited for a murder case. She sighed and contorted her face with disdain. "Mikros, wake me up when we about to land," she said before popping her ear buds in and closing her eyes.

Mikros tucked Adonis' mugshot away while thinking to himself, bitch please, you'd be the first one ready to sample that Mandingo.

Chapter 11

That same evening

7:32 pm

Jersey City, New Jersey

Chaz and Tonya had been going over Adonis' situation all day. They were dead set on trying to figure it out. They just couldn't believe what was going on. This wasn't supposed to be happening. Both women were extremely distraught. Especially Chaz, Adonis was all she had. Nothing or no one could fill the void that his absence bestowed upon her. Being informed of such devastation crippled her inability to think straight. All she wanted was for her husband to be home. Nothing else mattered. She wasn't even tripping about Tonya introducing herself as Adonis' girl. As long as Tonya did what needed to be done, Chaz was cool with playing her role.

Rep sat on the couch across from where the ladies sat, listening intensely as Tonya poured out her heart about Adonis. The way she was expressing her feelings to Chaz had Rep feeling like a trip to prison wouldn't be all that bad.

Rep's phone rang, it was Qua. "Yeah my nig, what's up?" he said after accepting the call.

"Yo you still at my mom's crib?"

"Trillz, like what's good?"

"A'ight, put my man's sister on the phone," Qua said with a bit of pain in his voice. He was heated that Lieutenant Moss did that bullshit to Monk, questioning if he'd be next once Adonis got transferred to Atlanta. Everybody knew that Qua and Adonis were close. So since Moss came at Monk like that, it was no telling what the faggot ass nigga would try with Qua.

"Here you go Chaz," Rep said as he got up to hand her the phone.

Chaz eyes lit up, she was hoping like hell Adonis called back before the night ended. "Hello," she spat anxiously after grabbing the phone.

"Yeah baby girl, what's up?" Adonis' voice came through the phone, sending a wave of emotions through his other half.

"I'm good I guess. Tonya was just letting me know what was going on. But listen Adonis, you need to grab a pencil and take down my number so when you get to Atlanta you can call me."

Adonis signaled for Qua to bring him something to write with. "A'ight, what's the number?"

"Four-seven-twelve-thirty-five-nine." Adonis quickly recognized the code she was sending him. "Girl you crazy, that number out of service. Give me the new number."

Chaz understood that he didn't want her to do what she was talking about doing, so she gave him her real cell phone number. Then she turned her attention towards Tonya as she spoke. "Oh yeah, your girlfriend is very pretty. You better hurry up home or I might take her from you," she said smiling at Tonya.

"You know the shit, I'm with it. But it's her husband with the ninety-nine problems," he said, letting her know that he wanted Moss dead. As well as being cool with the threesome she made reference of.

"I got you. Oh, and I'm leaving tonight to go back to Atlanta. I need to be down there."

"Naw, you stay where you at. I'll let you know when I need you to come down here."

"A'ight cool, but make sure you call me every chance you get. I love you," Chaz expressed.

"I love you more." Adonis announced then hung up.

Chaz handed Rep back his phone and the second he grabbed it Monique's number popped up as an incoming call. "Yeah, what you want?!!" Rep questioned with egotistic authority.

"I was just calling to say I'm sorry for what I did earlier. Now can you please come home?" Monique asked emotionally.

Rep looked across at the two sexy women that sat before him. He wanted so badly to sling dick to both of them. "Yeah, I'm on my way," he said with intentions of tearing Monique ass out the frame when he got home. "Yo Dee-Dee, I'm out!" he yelled from the living room after ending his call.

Dee-Dee came from the kitchen drying her hands on a towel. "Well it's about time. Shit, you been here all-day hounding for attention." She shot Chaz a sideways glance. "It ain't like you was gonna get some pussy anyway. Gon' and get ya wack ass out of here," Dee-Dee stated ill mannered.

Rep started laughing, "Yeah, I'm 'bout to leave. Looking at ya ugly ass just made me realize something."

"And what's that?" Dee-Dee asked while shooting him a hardened look.

"I just realized that I respect my dick too much to chase after something ya ugly ass had," he remarked then started toward the door.

"Well good, now respect this house and get the fuck out!" Dee-Dee expressed in her feelings.

Tonya sat there intrigued yet baffled by their little quarrel. She was a fiend for reality show type drama.

Rep flipped Dee-Dee the finger with his back to her. He wasn't beat to argue. Getting home to get his dick wet became his mission.

"Tonya, don't mind them. They always got some shit brewing. But anyway, what's this strategy you got to help my brother out? I know y'all gotta have something going on. I say that because he stay ten steps ahead of every situation." Chaz raked her hand through her hair while offering Tonya a sweet smile. "I mean, you must be doing something right. You got Adonis talking about he love you," she expressed as a ploy to play on Tonya's emotions.

A big silly smile blessed Tonya's face. She wasn't expecting for those words to come out of Chaz mouth. "He told you that he loved me?" Tonya asked, surprised.

"Let me guess, my brother ain't never tell you that he loved you?"

"I mean, well... Uhm." Tonya was searching for the right way to say no without looking stupid.

Chaz waved her off. "Girl that's just the way he is. He feels like he too macho for that shit. But I guess he told me 'cause he wanted me to know that you wasn't just some ole side chick." Chaz was laying it on thick. So thick in fact, Tonya's whole disposition changed. She lit up. Believing what Chaz had just told her was such a game changer.

"Well, to tell you the truth. I don't know what the plan is. All I know is, whatever Adonis say, that's what I'ma do. I just hope we can figure something out before the baby is born." Tonya placed her hand on her stomach.

Baby! Chaz screamed in her head while casting a fake ass smile. "Oh my God, you pregnant?" She asked joyfully as she scooted over to rub Tonya's belly. "Dee-Dee!" she yelled out.

Dee-Dee entered the living room, "What's up baby?"

"We about to be some aunties," expressed Chaz with her hand still on Tonya's stomach.

"Aww shit, Adonis done knocked that ass up. Talk about conjugal visits." Dee-Dee's joke enticed the trio to laugh. But internally, Chaz didn't find the situation to be funny. She felt as if she had been stabbed with a million knives of betrayal. Chaz only had two rules!And Adonis had just broke the first one.

"Well, you definitely family now. I guess you gonna have to accept the fact that you might be carrying a little serial killer. 'Cause my brother definitely put that work in," Chaz stated in a serious yet playful manner.

Tonya's brow went into a frown. She wasn't feeling Chaz's serial killing joke.

"Girl stop it," Dee-Dee said with a warm smile trying to keep Tonya from feeling uneasy. "Now y'all come on in here so we could eat. I done put together some official shit," Dee-Dee bragged as she led the way to the dining room.

***

As the ladies sat at the dining room table enjoying their succulent steak and shrimp dinner, Chaz was entertaining Tonya with stories about Adonis' upbringing. She painted a vivid picture. Taking Tonya down the road of Adonis' toughest years. Even Dee-Dee was getting a lesson on what it was like for him back in the day. At moments, Chaz would drop her eyes and speak in a low whisper as the shame, guilt and hurt from her and Adonis' growing pains promoted a heart aching agony. But Chaz wasn't alone in her feelings. Ironically, Dee-Dee and Tonya began to recap the moments in their childhood when their struggles were real.

"For the most part, those days are long gone," said Chaz with a renewed sense of confidence. "When my brother get home we gon' be good," she said enthusiastically.

"Chaz, that's a beautiful thought. I stay thinking about the day Adonis is released. I've never admired a man the way I admire him. He just got it working for him. Now I see where you get it from," Tonya spoke with glee.

Dee-Dee jerked her head back. "Tonya, do yourself a favor." Dee-Dee adopted a twisted look. "Don't get too comfortable. You might be fucking Adonis and carrying his baby, but that high yellow bitch right there belongs to me," she said pointing to Chaz.

Mr. Ish

Tonya threw her hands up, "My bad if I said something offensive. I was just saying—"

"Fuck what you were saying!" Dee-Dee got aggressive. "Did you hear what I said."

The fear that rose in Tonya's eyes could be seen by Stevie Wonder. She was petrified.

Chaz couldn't help but giggle. She always thought it was cute when Dee-Dee got gangsta for her boo. "Dee-Dee, knock it off!" Chaz stated. And when her and Dee-Dee eyes met they busted out laughing.

Tonya sighed with relief. She just knew Dee-Dee was about to fuck her up. "Girl you had me nervous as hell over here. I thought for sure you was about to kick my ass," Tonya stated with her hand over her heart.

Chaz poked a couple of shrimps onto her fork, "Dee-Dee was only messing with you. If anything, she'd eat ya ass, not kick it." Chaz popped the shrimps in her mouth with a slutty look in her eyes.

"Bitch, how you gonna say some shit like that. Just 'cause I suck farts out yo ass, don't mean I'll give every pretty bitch a rim job," Dee-Dee snapped back.

"Oh please, if Tonya was with it you'd have your face buried between her cheeks right now," replied Chaz reaching for her glass of juice. She took a sip. "Uhm, Tonya stand up real quick." Chaz got up and went around to the other side of the table to assist Tonya in standing. "Turn around," Chaz instructed in a warm tone.

Dee-Dee just shook her head. The thought of Chaz trying to wrap Tonya into a threesome started to beat on her brain.

"Now you mean to tell me you wouldn't eat her ass," Chaz pointed to Tonya's butt.

Tonya couldn't contain the laughter that jumped out of her throat, she was too amused.

"I'm saying, that shit is fat. But it might drop when she take those

67

pants off," Dee-Dee replied.

"You crazy," said Tonya spinning back around. "Ain't nothing sloppy about this booty." She rushed to wiggle her pants down, exposing a black laced thong. "I make sure I keep this shit tight," Tonya quoted before smacking her ass. She was confident that her ass measured up to the status quo.

"Damn Tonya, I know my brother love hitting you from the back," Chaz yelled as Tonya pulled her pants back up and sat down.

"You ain't lying," Tonya rebutted with swag. Then her phone vibrated. She glanced at the phone next to her plate. Of course it was Moss.

Chaz peeped the change in Tonya's face as she swiped the decline tag on the phone.

"Girl you better answer your phone. Your husband probably worried sick about you. You could at least let him know you're alright. I mean damn you been here all day without talking to him.

"Who said I'm married?" Tonya asked, unsure of what Chaz was getting at.

Chaz looked at Dee-Dee. "Baby we gon' have to teach Miss Suburbia how to have the best of both worlds." Then she turned her attention back to Tonya, "Look, when my brother told me he loved you, he also told me that he just hope when he come home you get a divorce."

Tonya ate that shit up like a starving child in a third world country. "A'ight, so how you think I should handle this? 'Cause there aint no room in my life for no other nigga except Adonis."

Chaz found it stimulating and sexy that another woman craved her husband with such strong desire. Only reinforcing in her head that Adonis was still the pick of the litter. No matter what his situation was.

"Yeah you say that shit, but are you really ready to prove that?" Chaz took another drink of her juice. "Because I ain't got no problem with proving my love when it comes to mine," she concluded while gazing over at Dee-Dee.

"Oh, so what you tryna to say," Tonya shot back on the defense.

"Girl, don't take it the wrong way. I was just saying that you got the best of both worlds right now. Even though you fucking with my brother, he can't do nothing for you right now. Truthfully, if you wanna have a future with Adonis you need to use your husband for everything he's worth."

"You know what." Tonya worked her hands like a hood-rat, "You're right, you are so right." Just then, her phone vibrated again.

"Tell that nigga something. Shit, tell him you on your way home and you can't wait to suck the skin off his dick," Chaz joked.

Tonya answered her phone, "Hey baby, what's up?"

"Where the hell you at, it's damn near nine o'clock and I've been tryna call you since I got off work," Moss erupted into the phone.

"Well, first of all, you need to calm down. I'm at my grandmother's house. You ain't even bother calling her phone. You know my grandma sick," Tonya emphasized.

"Yeah a'ight, you just make sure you get here when you done. Oh, and your little boyfriend's cellmate had a run in with a few of the guards at the prison. Just thought you should know," he told her just to get under her skin.

"Joseph, you need to stop it with all that boyfriend shit. Whoever got you believing that mess is who you need to be with. I'm your wife and I love you. Regardless if you get on my nerves or not."

Chaz gave Tonya the thumbs up. She liked the way Tonya personalized her feelings for Moss by calling him by his first name. That was a classic move.

Moss sat on the other end of that phone feeling like he was that dude. He was so self-absorbed, he never even considered the fact that Tonya was running game. "I love you too baby. I'll see you when you get home." he said and hung up.

Tonya looked at Chaz with the biggest smile ever. "Well, let me get up out of here. My husband is off tomorrow and I need to be at the prison to see Adonis before they take him to Atlanta." Tonya stood up to leave.

"Alright then." Chaz stood up as well. "Here, take my number so we can stay in touch. 'Cause I'm telling you now, Adonis gonna have us jumping through hoops for his ass. I just hope you built for the shit that he's gonna need us to do," explained Chaz while giving Tonya a hug.

"A'ight now, y'all pretty bitches could stop all that hugging and let go," Dee-Dee interrupted.

The ladies broke their embrace. Tonya stepped back and looked at Chaz with tears welling in her eyes. "Chaz," she paused to collect herself. "I don't care what it is Adonis need me to do. If it's gonna help get him home, then I'll do whatever. And I mean that shit!" she said in all seriousness.

Chapter 12

Fulton County Jail (Atlanta)

10:03 pm That same night

"Yo, you's a stinking ass nigga," Flex said to New York. "If I knew you'd be farting like this I would of never let yo ass move in my cell."

Flex laid in his bunk with his shirt covering his nose. It was just awful the way New York smelled. He smelled as if his insides were rotten. "Fuck!" Flex screamed, mad as ever.

New York struggled not to let Flex hear him on the top bunk laughing. For some strange reason, he found it hilarious whenever he passed gas. Its only been a couple days that they've been cellmates, and Flex was already regretting that he let New York move in his cell.

"Next time you gotta bust yo ass, sit on the toilet and flush that shit. Or, we gonna be up in this bitch rocking!" Flex stated aggressively. And no sooner than he spoke, New York hopped out his bunk to flush a fart. Flex looked at him like he was the nastiest motherfucker known to man. "Fuck you grinning for? Ain't nothing funny," Flex ranted.

Still, New York laughed. He just couldn't control his inner child.

Flex got up out his bunk, "Dig this, either you gonna start respecting me up in here, or I'ma play by your rules and we gonna be up in this bitch acting a fool together. You wanna play games? 'Cause if that's the case I'll start beating my dick whenever I feel like it."

New York's smile turned upside down. "Yeah a'ight, don't play with me like that. Try that shit if you want to. I'ma knock yo ass out," he told Flex before standing up and getting in his face.

Flex took a step back. "See how mad you got when I started talking craziness. All I'm saying is, we both grown as hell, a little respect goes a long way."

New York never responded. He climbed back in his bunk with anger still flowing through his veins. At which point, the sadistic sexaul sadist within him, was on its way to being resurrected. Then the thought of stripping Flex of his manhood caressed his brain. An image of Flex begging for mercy flashed through his head. Followed by a slideshow of his previous sex crimes. And among that slideshow was the foul shit he did to his niece Chaz when she was a child. Tyrone Newsome A.K.A. New York—was as sick as they came. The nigga euphoria levels begin to rise. He could feel the difference in his body chemistry. His urge to do Flex dirty became an internal battle. Nevertheless, he fought back his feelings. "Only if this nigga knew I'd rip his asshole open," he mumbled in a whisper to himself.

"Huh!" Flex asked stupidly.

"I ain't say nothing. I was just up here praying," New York replied.

***

At the same time, back in New Jersey

Adonis sat on his bunk flicking back and forth through the

channels on his TV. He wasn't necessarily looking for anything specific. Though he couldn't sleep and wanted to keep his mind off of the three situations that were stressing him out: Monk, Chaz and Atlanta. Of course there wasn't anything on the TV worth watching. South Woods had the shittiest stations out of all the prisons in Jersey. Frustration began to set in. He shut the TV off. "Damn Monk! Don't worry bro, I'ma hold you down, that faggot ass nigga gonna get his. I put that on my dick, I got that nigga!" Adonis spoke out loud to himself. This was his last night in South Woods and he hated every second of it. He couldn't wait to get to the Fulton County Jail. Although, he would have preferred to hit the streets.

Adonis got up and grabbed a pen and paper. He always used writing as an outlet whenever life's problems began to pile up. Even on the street, writing was sort of like therapy for him. It was his way of getting his issues out of his head. Initially, he started jotting down different ways he'd love to kill a number of people. The more he wrote, the more people he added to his list. Periodically a smile would make a guest appearance whenever certain names popped up in his head. He even took it back to wanting to kill a kid that had gotten the best of him in the fourth grade.

After about two pages in, he grew tired of raking his brain for names. "All you motherfuckers can die slow," he growled as he ripped the papers up. Shortly after, he climbed back in his bunk. But still, he couldn't sleep. His restlessness was getting the best of him. That's when the beautiful images of Chaz and Tonya walked into his head. "Damn, I gotta get the fuck home!" he stated to himself clicking the TV back on. SportsCenter, he thought as he turned to ESPN. Ironically, the station had no signal.

"Davis," said the C.O. tapping on Adonis' cell door.

Adonis looked at the guard with a killer stare. He was hoping like hell they tried coming up in there on some bullshit. He was ready, and it showed in his eye's.

Element of Surprise II

"You're being transferred to Atlanta in the morning, be sure to have your personal things ready," the C.O. told him.

"Yeah, I know," Adonis replied. And then his mind started traveling to places it had no business. He caught himself. Again, he got out his bunk and grabbed a piece of paper and a pen. Leaving Qua a letter of gratitude seemed appropriate. After all, that's what his character consisted of.

> *Yo Qua,*
>
> *By the time you get this letter I should be on my way to ATL. But don't even trip my nigga, a part of me will always be right here with you. I've come to love you like a brother and nothing could ever change that. As you can see, I am a genuine dude. My respect for you is off the charts and I am forever indebted to you. I'm pretty sure you understand my reasoning for not telling you that Chaz was my sister. However, I don't think I could ever repay you or your mother for keeping her safe. That girl means the world to me and she's all I have. I just want you to know that I appreciate the authenticity you've shared with me throughout these years. Because as we both know, this spot is filled with fronting, lying ass niggas.*
>
> *Qua you are gifted in a lot of ways. You have qualities that only fake niggas dream about. I just hope and pray that your appeal goes through, because our society needs a soldier like you to lead those who are misguided. I got nothing but love for you.*
>
> *Also, I'ma need you to focus on staying clear of that nigga Moss. I don't need for you to get all jammed up for the way he feels about me. After all, you weren't the one fucking his wife, I was! Yeah nigga, I was fucking the social worker. How's that for moving real right, (ha-ha). Anyway, I'ma hit you when I touch ATL and let you know the status of my situation.*
>
> *One love,*
> *Adonis*

74

Mr. Ish

P.S. Get ya game up!

Adonis folded the letter up and stuck it in an envelope. Then he climbed in his bunk and closed his eyes. Moments later, he was fast asleep.

***

Meanwhile
Back in ATL

New York stood a few feet away from Flex. Naked, with his dick greased and ready. His mouth began to water as he looked down at Flex laying on his stomach. Gently, he stroked his meat to the protruding lump of Flex's ass, poking up underneath the blanket. The more he stroked himself, the greater his craving to fuck Flex in the asshole increased.

Flex must have felt his presence. Out of nowhere he jumped up. "Yo what the fu—

New York's fist cut Flex's startled question short. Boom! Boom! Pow! New Yorks Primitive desire to rape Flex had just reached it's pinacle.

Flex struggled to fight as best he could, but New York was just too strong. Then he managed to get Flex in a choke-hold. Instantly, Flex began to fade out. He started wheezing, gasping and slapping. Though it was pointless. New York wanted that booty, and by all means, he was about to get it. He licked Flex's ear, "I'ma love fucking yo lil frail ass," he said in a grunt as he threw Flex down.

Flex crashed hard to the concrete, face first with his narrow ass tooted in the air.

"Somebody must'a told this nigga what my favorite position is," New York said laughing, just before ripping Flex boxers away. Then it happened, Tyrone 'New York' Newsome commenced to violate Michael 'Flex' Owens in the worst way. Like a raging bull New York non-remorsefully plunged into that nigga's dooky shoot. Upon impact, Flex's eyes shot open and he began screaming. Yet his cries and yells only excited the sadistic maniac. Harder and stronger, New York pumped in and out, enjoying every stroke. Helplessly, Flex just laid there. He didn't even have the strength to fight for his manhood anymore. It was as if he had given up.

After New York was done, he climbed off of Flex with his dick saturated in blood and shit. "Now get your bitch ass up and clean out your asshole. You my bitch now. So I'ma need you to stay clean for daddy!" New York bellowed gruelingly.

Chapter 13

Philadelphia airport,

Friday morning

Finally, Mikros and Erica arrived at the airport. It took them forever to get there. What started out as a delay ended in a full cancellation and they had to reboard a different flight. Nonetheless, they were where they needed to be. Once outside, they were greeted by two New Jersey State Troopers who would assist them in getting to the prison to get Adonis.

"Girl, I just love me a man in uniform," Mikros said to Erica as they approached the troopers. Erica couldn't help but roll her eyes. She had no idea that Mikros was so annoying. Had she known he was this aggravating, she would have stayed with the Special Victims' Unit.

"Hello, I'm Trooper Williams and this is my partner Miles," said the taller of the two State Troopers while extending his hand.

"Uhm," Mikros murmured. "I'm Mikros. This here is Detective Sykes," Mikros said in rare manly tone while shaking Williams hand.

"Pleasure to meet you both. Mikros you ride with me. Sykes, youcould ride with Miles. It's protocol that we use two vehicles when extraditing a suspect or prisoner across state lines," explained Williams.

"Right, and you can call me Erica. No need to be so formal," she said while trailing the Trooper who seemed to be in a rush.

Thoughtlessly, Erica looked out the window as Trooper Miles drove across the Ben Franklin Bridge into New Jersey. She could feel him lustfully glancing over at her. She paid him no mind. She just wanted to get to the prison, get Adonis, and get back to Atlanta.

"So, I hear your suspect commited his murder over fifteen years ago?" Miles inquired.

"Not sure if he's guilty." Erica's response was dry and a bit cold.

Miles caught her drift and cut on the radio. He switched to a Country station. "I hope you don't mind," he said as he turned up the volume.

Erica sighed in disgust as Garth Brooks lyrics assaulted her eardrums. Only confirming her initial assumption of Trooper Miles being a black hillbilly.

Nonetheless, there was an altogether different story going on with Trooper Williams and Mikros during their commute. The two were just as talkative as a couple of high school students. And for a couple of dudes just meeting each other, they sure felt comfortable in their discussion.

"Now you mean to tell me that your cousin influenced your sexual preference?" Trooper Williams asked.

Mikros kind of had this thing with him where he'd try to get people to understand why he was gay. He rationalized in his head that being gay was the only way of life. Hoping one day the world would see things the way he sees them. "I'm not gonna say he influenced me, I'd just say he opened my eyes to the truth. You acting all macho and shit, but I'm pretty sure the thought of fucking a man crossed your mind before."

Williams swerved hard and pulled over, bringing the car to a screeching halt. He turned to face Mikros. "Man, what the fuck is wrong with you! Ain't no real man gonna be thinking about fucking another man in the ass. Now it's best you stay quiet for the remainder of the ride, or I'ma give you more than what you're looking for!" Williams shouted with his face severely twisted.

Mikros was scared out of his wits. He hadn't expected for Williams to flip out like that. Evidently, Williams was nowhere near susceptible to the seed Mikros called himself trying to plant.

Shamed face, Mikros kept silent and looked out the window as Williams drove on. That was the story of his life. Every time he tried to get someone to understand his way of thinking, the more he was frowned upon. But for some reason, he never wavered in trying to get his point across.

***

Meanwhile, back in Jersey
South Woods State Prison

Adonis sat in the holding cell in the intake area waiting for his escorts to arrive. He had been there since seven-thirty and it was now going on ten o'clock. But if he didn't have anything else, he had patience.

Tonya entered the intake area with no regard for the opinions of others. Stepping with a purpose, she made her way over to the holding cell where Adonis was. "Wait a minute," she said holding up one finger before going to get the guard to open the cell door.

Adonis stood up and posted in a b-boy stance against the wall. His confidence—even as a nigga in extreme circumstances—spoke volumes. As soon as the door buzzed open Adonis walked out. Tonya signaled for him to come to the back office. Her gesture was borderline demanding.

In stride, Adonis smirked to himself as the lumps of Tonya's ass jiggled in her pink velour sweatpants. Damn I'ma miss that soft ass, he thought as he trailed her into the office. And no sooner than they crossed the threshold of the office, the guard yelled out for Adonis.

"Have a seat," insisted Tonya as she went to inform the guard that Adonis had some papers to sign. That was her number one go to line whenever she needed to get him alone for a few minutes. Once out on the open floor, she spotted the Troopers and the two Atlanta Detectives. Her heart sank as the reality of Adonis being taken away from her began to set in. Although she knew there was nothing she could do to stop it, it was the overall situation that had her feeling like life couldn't have been crueler.

"He'll be out in just a minute, I have some papers for him to sign," Tonya explained without making eye contact. Quickly, she walked back to the office and shut the door. "Adonis, I love you so much," she whined with a face full of tears as she practically jumped into Adonis' lap.

Affectionately, he embraced her. He could tell she was truly hurting. "Shh," he whispered compassionately. "It's alright baby. I just need you to follow my instructions once I find out what's going on. We good baby, believe me. We good! I just need you to be strong and hold on," he expressed with an optimized certainty.

Tonya's face rested in the crook of his neck. He could feel her warm, panting breath getting hotter with each sob.

"You hear me baby? Just stay strong." He kissed her forehead and slowly broke his embrace.

Tonya stood up, trying to rid herself of the tears that dripped from her eyes. This was perhaps one of the most difficult things she had ever been faced with, but she had already made her mind up. She was gonna stay strong, do whatever needed to be done and see to it that Adonis made it home. Nothing was gonna stop her. In her heart he loved her. In her mind she needed him, and in her stomach, was a part of him.

Adonis moved her hands away from her face, "I love you baby," he said before kissing her.

Mr. Ish

"Stop!" She pulled away and stood up. "Just go Adonis, go!" she said as she struggled to fight back her tears. She just couldn't bear to see him get put in cuffs. "I gotta go. Call me when you get settled in," she said in a low painful tone before turning and walking out the door.

For the first time, Adonis felt something for Tonya—be it love or sympathy—but he felt something. Moreover, he didn't have time to marinate in his feelings. He had to get his ass to Atlanta so he could work on getting home. So with the determination of getting the shit over and done with, he made his way over to the ATL Detectives. There was no sense in procrastinating the inevitable any longer.

"Davis, go wait over there, Detective Mikros will be with you shortly," instructed the C.O. in charge of Adonis' discharge.

As Adonis walked to the holding area, Mikros couldn't help but blatantly gawk at him.

"Knock it off," Erica growled through clenched teeth as she nudged Mikros. "As a matter of fact, Trooper Williams, can you do me a favor and search the prisoner and get him ready for transport. The last thing we need is for Mikros to get his ass kicked," Erica said while laughing.

"Ha-ha very funny," Mikros mumbled with attitude. But that was about as far as he went with his rebuttal. He knew what Erica said was dead on point. It was clear to see that Adonis would have kicked his ass.

Trooper Williams didn't object to helping out. Anything to speed up the process and get away from Mikros. Within minutes, Adonis was searched, shackled and ready for extradition. Williams walked Adonis to the exit window to be identified, then to the car as Mikros and Erica handled the last of the paperwork. About five minutes later, they were back enroute to Philadelphia International Airport.

"Mr. Davis, its been a long time since I've seen you. We have a lot to talk about," said Mikros as if he and Adonis were the best of friends.

"We ain't got shit to talk about. My native tongue is lawyer, not pig latin!"

Mikros adjusted the rearview mirror so he could see Adonis as he spoke, "Well, you could speak whatever language you want, but when we get to Atlanta you better learn how to speak plea bargain. 'Cause if not, your pretty yellow ass will never make it home."

Adonis never responded, he had no reason to. Though once he figured it all out, he be damned if he wasn't gonna maneuver his way back to freedom.

***

Later on that day, Down in Atlanta

When Neesha got to work that Friday afternoon, she was shocked to hear that Flex had been raped by New York. It was no secret that New York was a sicko, but no one expected him to be a booty bandit. Neesha was stunned to hear such devastating news. All she could think about was telling Erica.

Neesha's stomach churned as she read the reports about the damage New York caused Flex. In layman terms, he had ripped Flex's asshole wide open. Then she read that Flex was transported to an off grounds hospital. At that point she couldn't stand to read anymore.

Neesha closed the logbook and insisted on taking her break early. This was something she couldn't keep to herself. First, she called Pike. "Hey baby what you doing?" she asked the second he answered.

"Nothing much, I was about to text you and ask you for the pin number on your bank card 'cause I forgot it."

"1984," she said without a second thought. "But listen baby, I was calling to tell you that your people's Flex got raped by his bunky. They took him to the hospital."

"What! What you mean he got raped, like fucked in the butt?" Pike asked in befuddlement.

"Uhm hmm, yeah. I had went to his unit to drop off that package you gave me and that's when I found out."

"A'ight yo, find out what's up with that nigga New York and I'll see you tonight."

"A'ight baby. And don't be riding around with a bunch of niggas in my car either."

"Girl, knock it off. When you stop running from this dick, then I'll consider giving you some lead way to put your foot down. But until then, I'm running the show. Understand me," Pike stated full of himself.

"Yes daddy, I hear that hot shit," Neesha stated with a lustful tone before hanging up. She was all in when it came to Pike's young ass. Even though she still hadn't gave him the pussy. However, she wasn't oppose to letting the nigga eat that box and butthole. Anyway, she needed to call Erica and inform her of the nasty foul shit New York did.

Erica's phone vibrated on her hip as she sat alone behind Adonis, on the plane. Sitting next to Mikros wasn't even an option for her. "Hold on," Erica said when she answered then went to the restroom to take the call. "Yeah girl, what's up?" she asked while locking the stall door.

"Please tell me you back in Atlanta, 'cause oh my god! That sick bastard Tyrone Newsome done raped his bunky."

"What!" screamed Erica. She just knew her ears were deceiving her. It was no way she was hearing her right.

"Yes girl, that twisted ass nigga done raped Flex."

"Flex?" Erica questioned. Instantly she recognized the name. "Are you talking about Michael Owens?"

"You know him?" Neesha asked, not surprised by the possibility.

"Yeah, I know him. As a matter of fact, the guy I just picked up in Jersey is the one that killed Flex brother back in the day. Damn, I feel bad for him. So where is Flex now, and what happen to Tyrone?"

"Well, Flex is in the hospital and Tyrone is in lock-up."

"A'ight then, I'll call you tonight. I got some stuff to handle. But now you see what I was talking about when I told you that Tyrone need to be dealt with," Erica concluded then hung up. That psycho need to be castrated, she thought as she unlocked the restroom. When she got back to her seat she couldn't help but notice that Adonis was humming the lyrics to TLC's classic song, WaterFalls. That was her jam growing up. Not to mention, the song that she lost her virginity to. Instantly, she was taken back to a place when life was less stressful and problematic. "Mr. Davis what you know about that song," she said as she sat down. But Adonis didn't reply, he just continued to hum while staring out the window. It was obvious that he didn't wanna socialize. Because despite Erica's sweet voice and stout urban assets, the bitch was still a cop. So in his eyes, she was only worthy of dying a horrific death.

Mikros turned around, "Sykes, let's switch seats for a bit. I can barely keep my eyes open,"

That's when Adonis decided to comment, "Yeah detective, could you please switch seats with this bone smuggling cracker."

"Oh!" Erica threw her hands up to her mouth. That was the last thing she was expecting to hear.

Mikros hissed and rolled his eyes, "Come on girl switch with me," he said getting out his seat.

Still amused to no end Erica got up and swapped seats with Mikros. Thus the minute she sat down next to Adonis, her heart fluttered like a school girl experiencing her first crush. She even felt a tingle in her pussy.

Adonis looked over at her and immediately thought about fucking her beautiful face. Then he dismissed the thought just as fast as it entered his head. He turned his attention back to the sunny, blue sky. It was beautiful. "Damn!" slipped out his mouth in frustration. He had just served five years and now this. What a disappointment.

The plane began to experience turbulence. Off of reflex, Erica grabbed Adonis wrist. She gasped deeply.

"You alright?" Adonis asked out of concern.

Immediately, Erica snatched her hand back. "Yeah, I'm good. I was just checking your handcuffs. Are they too tight?" she questioned with no hesitation.

Adonis wasn't buying it. And she could tell. Moreover, Erica stood and retrieved her leather carrying bag from the overhead compartment. Getting back to Tyrone's file became her addiction. She carried that file with her at all times. Her obsession with getting at the sadistic bastard took up the majority of her brain space. She couldn't go a full thirty minutes without thinking about the million and one ways she'd love to murder him.

Erica opened the binder, reading over the same material she had read countless times before. It seemed as if she just loved to torture herself. Because outside of walking into the Fulton County Jail and putting a bullet inside Tyrone's head, there was nothing else she could do.

The pilot's voice came over the intercom, informing the passengers to prepare and brace for landing. Erica went to close the folder. At which point, Adonis glanced over. The impact of what he saw felt like a thousand knives penetrating his chest. "What the fuck you doing with that picture of Tyrone!" he said with unprecedented anger. His words were saturated with malicious hatred.

"You know him?" Erica asked inquisitively.

Adonis' nose flared as it often did whenever he was upset. Chaz's face popped into his head. Followed by the horrific stories she had told him, regarding Tyrone's molestation of her. Vividly, he could recall the pain in Chaz's voice, and the hurt in her eyes as she told him—many years ago—what her uncle did to her when she was a child.

Adonis took a deep breath. "Nah, I don't know him," he answered. Despite how bad he wanted to snatch Tyrone's heart out, he wasn't about to compromise his integrity by working with the police.

Erica knew Adonis was lying. The magnitude of his initial outburst raised many red flags. Her mind began racing. She didn't know what was going on. Never would she have fathomed the thought of the two of them knowing each other. She tried to get a read on Adonis' body language, but it was too late. He had already decompressed. It served him no purpose in getting himself worked up at the moment. He had his own issues to deal with.

Desperate to do something, anything that might help her get Tyrone, Erica grabbed Adonis' arm. "Mr. Davis please," she sighed anxiously, glancing back to see if Mikros was paying attention. Yet Mikros was still asleep. Adonis peered in her eyes as if to say—bitch get the fuck off me. But his aggressive stare didn't deter her. "We can help each other!" she pleaded with him.

Adonis leaned in close. His lips were only inches from hers. Then he snarled before saying, "It ain't nothing you could help me with. Now leave me the fuck alone, you cop ass bitch!"

Chapter 14

Friday afternoon,

South Woods State Prison

Qua was elated after reading the letter that Adonis had slid under his door before he left. He couldn't believe Adonis was fucking Tonya. That new-found information was one for the ages. Yet, Qua could do nothing but respect the fact that his boy led by example when it came to moving like an official nigga is supposed to move. Even in the absence of his comrade, he was still being schooled.

Qua put the letter up and went to cover the window of his cell door for a little privacy. He had to take a shit, and he wasn't a fan of Nigga's peeking in on him as they passed. After prepping the chrome throne, he got right to it. His bowels were screaming to be released. "Whoa!" he exhaled as he flushed in a failed attempt to keep the smell down. The mixture of prison food and canteen was the worst combination in the wolrd. Diarrhea was often the result. All of five minutes later and he was done. After wiping his ass and washing his hands, he grabbed his radio and put the beats on. Mellowing out for the remainder of the day became his game plan. It wasn't often that he took time out for himself. However with Adonis gone, the fucked up feelings of being left there alone started to weigh him down. So relaxing at that point gave him the chance to gather his thoughts. Although he wasn't the type to isolate, he still needed to put things into perspective. Most of which consisted of getting an answer on his appeal. Going home stayed at the forefront of his mind. Yet, most of the jokers he kicked it with didn't even know about the dilemmas that he faced. Mainly because he so often exercised a carefree attitude. But that was just his way of dealing with things.

Just as Qua began to zone out, his bunky came dragging his raggedy ass in the cell. Qua looked at the nigga with his face twisted. Every sighting of his celly got him angry. He truly hated that dude. Qua hopped out his bunk and put on his sneakers to go out to the rec room. There was no way he could stay in the cell without wanting to fuck his bunky up. His vibe had just been killed.

On his way to the rec room, Tonya walked onto his unit. She came to see a few of the inmates that signed up to ask her a bunch of dumb ass questions. Honestly, they just wanted a little attention.

Qua walked over to her office. Although he wasn't on the list, he figured he'd shoot in and rap with her before a line of vultures formed outside her door.

"Hey Mrs. Jackson, can I have a word with you?" Qua asked standing in the doorway.

"Yeah of course. Have a seat Mr. Mason," she said as she situated herself.

Qua sat, noticing the lack of sleep in her eyes. But he didn't comment. He just basically wanted to see what type of vibe she'd give off being as though Adonis was no longer there.

"So, what's on your mind Mr. Mason," she asked without making eye contact.

"Nothing much, Adonis told me to tell you something before he left." Qua threw Adonis name in the mix just to see her reaction.

There was a slight pause in her movement as she carried on with situating her log book and sign in sheet. "Adonis?" She acted surprised. "Mr. Mason, what are you talking about," she said still not making eye contact.

A light chuckle escaped him. "I feel you on that. It ain't like y'all thing was being blasted around the prison. You know my boy kept to himself."

By this point he had her full attention. She looked at him with piercing eyes and a disgruntled expression.

Though he wasn't fooled by her act. He knew Adonis wasn't the type to front, lie or say shit just for acceptance. "Well anyway, he told me to let you know that if any of these niggas in here disrespect you, for you to let me know." He flashed a charismatic smile. "And I'll take care of it."

"Mr. Mason, I appreciate you giving me this alleged message from your friend, but I have the slightest idea about what you're talking about. Now if you'll excuse me, I got guys waiting to be seen."

Tonya wasn't falling for the okie doke. Part of the reason she fucked with Adonis in the first place was because he didn't move like the average joker. Plus, she knew Adonis was gonna be contacting her soon, so she didn't wanna confirm anything without speaking to him first. It was imperative that she played things cautiously. The last thing she wanted to do was throw herself under the bus.

"A'ight den, I guess we done here." Qua stood up to leave, "And just to let you know, Adonis ain't gone let that shit that your husband did to his bunky ride. But, you ain't hear that from me," he expressed while giggling. Then he made his way over to the phone to call Rep.

Still, Tonya didn't feed. She was not about to confirm or deny anything.

As per-usual, Rep didn't answer until the second time Qua called. Apparently, he was too busy skeeting jism down Monique's throat. "Yeah, what's good my boy?" Rep asked after accepting the call.

"Same fight, different round. So, what up with you?" Qua ain't really have much to talk about, he was just basically looking to pass time until lock in.

"Shit, did Atlanta come and get ya boy?" Asked Rep walking naked towards the living room to light his blunt.

"Yeah, they came and got him this morning. Son was an official nigga, real talk," Qua spewed emotionally. It was evident that he missed his right hand man.

"Yeah, baby girl came by your mom's house yesterday to see his sister. That's a bad bitch son." Rep exhaled the weed smoke. "Shit, her fine ass had a nigga thinking that a trip to the bean couldnt be all that bad. Especially if all them broads coming like that."

Instantly, Qua directed his attention towards Tonya's office. Computing what Rep had just told him changed the game. "You talking about the bitch whose name starts with a T right?" Qua asked just to be sure he wasn't thinking the wrong shit.

"Yes sir, thats that bitch. She came up in there wearing all that ass. Just thinking about that bitch get a nigga dick hard," Rep said.

"TMI my nigga I'll holla at you later." Qua hung the phone up. A slight smirk caressed his mouth, inspired by the thought of the social worker sitting in his living room. Just as he attempted to step in her direction, the C.O. announced that it was lock-in time. He rushed over to the doorway of her office. He looked as if he wanted to inform the whole world that she was at his house yesterday. Steadfast, he shot in front of the next guy in line. He entered and shut the door behind him. His disrespect was always on a million.

"Oh yeah, I almost forgot. Adonis also told me to tell you he said thanks for going to see his sister yesterday," Qua expressed with a shitty smirk.

Tonya couldn't deny it any further, hook line and sinker. Qua had her. She was caught red handed, and her body language confirmed it. Then Qua broke back in to seal the deal. "Shit, I'm surprised my god-sister Dee-Dee didn't try and holla at you." He laughed then added, "I gotta lock in. I'll see you later," he stated before stepping off.

Tonya sat there dumbfounded. She had no words. Ironically though, she did feel appreciated and loved. Only Adonis could make her feel this way, even in his absence. She was too thrilled. Hearing that Adonis told another man that he appreciated her, warmed her heart. But only if she knew...

When Tonya got back to the Administration Building, she wondered if Adonis had been processed into the Fulton County Jail. It was nearing three o'clock and his flight had landed about two hours ago. She dug into her handbag and retrieved her cell phone. Calling Chaz seemed like the fastest way to find out the status of Adonis' situation. If anybody knew anything, it would most definitely be Chaz. Tonya's leg shook rapidly as she eagerly waited for Chaz to answer the phone. To no avail, it went to voicemail. "Damn this," she said then went to her computer to google the phone number for the Fulton County Jail. She was determined to find out what was going on with him. By the time it was all said and done, she had it all. She had even gotten his exact location, all the way down to his cell number. As soon as she confirmed that he had been processed in, she logged on to the Fulton County Jail website and put three hundred dollars on his books. She wasn't about to have her man going without. Although Chaz was more than capable of holding him down, Tonya felt it was her duty to make sure he didn't need for nothing.

After making sure Adonis was good Tonya gathered her things to leave. She was exhausted. Operating off of two hours of sleep in the last forty-eight hours really dug into her. But it was all worth it in her eyes. On the way to her car she felt her phone vibrate in the bag, which was hooked onto her shoulder. Moss, she thought while unlocking the car. She knew it was him because he made it a habit to call her as soon as she got off work. Being a pest was like his signature way of living. So much so, she didn't even care to call him back. Tonya was so far removed from having feelings for Moss, it was a shame.

During her drive home, she could barely keep her eyes open. Luckily, she didn't live too far from the prison. Tonya pulled into her driveway, parking alongside Moss' black F-150. The thought of relaxing and unwinding became her best friend. Yet, that thought was quickly dismissed the moment she entered the house. She totally felt disconnected from the place she called home. A stranger in familiar territory would best describe the feelings that came over her. Once inside,she discovered the lifeless body of her husband —lying face down on the living room floor—saturated in his own blood.

Tonya froze. Her heart sank as the trauma of what she saw left her stupefied. Even if she had attempted to scream, it would have been a silent one. But there was no attempt made. Mannequin like, she stared in a daze as if she was daydreaming. Suddenly, Chaz appeared out of nowhere eating a turkey and cheese sandwich that she had just made moments ago.

"Girl, I didn't even hear you come in. Let me find out you something like a ninja," Chaz said snickering.

Still in disbelief over what laid before her, Tonya was held captive. She was non-responsive.

Chaz approached, calm as could be while eating her sandwich. She was truly a heartless bitch. "Uhm." Chaz swallowed. "You need to stop it with all that white girl—'Oh my God, I'm in shock'— bullshit." She stepped in closer. Now face to face with Tonya. "Look, everything is good. Trust me! This is not my first rodeo when it comes to this murder game." Chaz shifted her weight. Standing semi-hood ratish while waving her sandwich in Tonya's face. "Bitch you better get it together. Now I told you when you came to see me that shit was gonna get real. Guess what? Shit don' got real. Now I ain't sure how you're used to operating, but when it comes to family, we go hard for one another. And I be damned if I let that nigga stand in the way." Chaz pointed at Moss' dead body then took another bite of her sandwich. "Now go and do whatever it is you was about to do and let me finish handling my business," she stated as she turned and walked back in the kitchen.

Something Chaz said must have awakened Tonya's darkside. There was a slow change in her body language. Her face lit up and joy danced in her eyes. Automatically, Tonya's mind wrapped itself around Adonis and her unborn child. Overwhelmed with the excitement of being free from her marriage, Tonya walked over to where Moss' body laid. Careful not to step in his blood, she kneeled down as close as possible. "And by the way." She smiled devilishly, "I was fucking Adonis, and I'm about to have his baby."

***

Two in a half hours earlier

Dee-Dee pulled up and parked about three houses down from Tonya's house. It was time for her and Chaz to pay Moss a visit. Carrying out Adonis' orders to kill the maggot of a man appealed to them both. Not that either of them had anything better to do with their time anyway.

After assessing their surroundings, the time had come. Chaz stepped out of the car wearing a white tennis skirt with a pink and gray halter top. She needed to show as much skin as possible if she wanted to get Moss' nasty ass to play into her little game.

Dee-Dee waited for Chaz to start towards the house then pulled off. She didn't need the nosy residents in the neighborhood focusing their attention on the unfamiliar vehicle lurking about.

Chaz cut her eyes at Dee-Dee as she drove off. Giving her a seductive—'naughty girl'—glance.

"I swear her pretty ass lucky I love her," Dee-Dee stated while turning the corner.

Even In the process of going to commit a murder, Chaz could have graced the cover of any prominent magazine. Everything about her creamed sex appeal. From her bronzed sun tan, all the way down to her toned, sleek legs. Even her neck was sexy. Moreover, it was her well rounded ass and flat stomach that put her over the top. Not to mention, she walked with class and contentment. As if being a bad bitch was her culture.

Just before reaching the driveway, Chaz stopped to purposely untie the laces on her right sneaker. She had on a pair of pink, white, and gray Air Max 95s. Then she stood erect and made her way to the door.

"Ding Dong," the doorbell sounded off. There was no answer. Nothing! She rang the bell again.

"Who is it!" Moss bellowed as he power stepped downstairs. The tenor of his voice was deep though scratchy, as if he had just woken up. Chaz didn't respond.

"Who is it?" Moss questioned again while looking out the peephole.

Chaz was just about to give her name when the door opened. "Hello, my name is Chantell. I have some information that you might be interested in hearing," she expressed while working her face luringly.

Moss gave her a weary look. "Information? What information?" he asked aggressively.

Chaz moaned lightly. "Uhm, this sun is beaming," she said in a sensual tone. Suddenly, she got stern. "Listen, it's too hot out here for me to be getting grilled by you and the sun," she stated prior to morphing into the ghetto version of her sexy self. "Tonya is your wife!" Chaz pointed her finger at him. "If you wanna know who she fucking then ask her. But I'll tell you this, you ain't gone never find out with that type of attitude." Chaz snaked her neck and turned as if she was about to leave.

"Ah, oh wait a minute," Moss called out, stopping her in her tracks.

Chaz struggled not to laugh as she turned back to face him.

What!" she said smacking her lips.

"Why don't you come on in so we could get to the bottom of this," Moss said then continued, "It ain't no need for you to be out here in this heat like this."

Chaz rolled her eyes, her front game was on a million. Especially when it came to getting her way. With a fake smile she entered. She was a beast at getting her way. Moss closed the door behind them. When he turned around, Chaz was bent at the waist tying her shoelace. She stood with her feet together, giving him a preview of her protruding pussy— which poked out like a ripe Georgia peach. "Damn!" he said openly.

Chaz looked back and grinned. "I know right, my pussy fat as hell," she blurted out then stood up to face him. "I was gonna wear some panties, but I wanted to let my kitty get some air," she giggled girlishly.

Moss nodded his head, pushing his lips into an agreeable frown. "A'ight cool, right this way." He led Chaz to the living room. After they sat, he drove right into interrogation mode. "So, what is it exactly you gotta tell me?" he questioned from the couch opposite of where she sat.

"Well, to be honest with you. Your wife is fucking my husband. Now am I mad? Hell yeah, but it's cool though," Chaz spoke with her hands like the hood-rats of the world. "Cause I gotta plan for the both of them."

"Hold on, did you just tell me that my wife is fucking your husband." Moss couldn't believe what he was hearing.

"Yeah, that's what I said. At first, I was gonna shoot that bitch in the head. Then I found out she was married. So I was like fuck it. I might as well come over here and give you some pussy," she giggled enticingly.

"Well, listen Chantell. I appreciate you coming to me with this information. Now is there some way you could prove what you're saying. 'Cause I'ma be honest with you, if that's the case, then we need to confront them both. And as far as us fucking, I aint about that life. My wife is all the woman I need." Moss then gave her a simple look. "And how did you know where we lived at, anyway?"

"Hum, you could blame Google for the address. As far as proof goes, that's gonna be kind of hard to produce since my husband is in Georgia." Chaz looked at her watch. "Well, he should be in Georgia by now."

"Georgia? Y'all live in Georgia?" he asked totally clueless as to what she was talking about.

Chaz jerked her eyebrows thinking to herself how stupid Moss was. Totally off topic she cupped her breast. "You think I got some pretty titties?" she asked, lifting up her shirt.

"Look Chantell, I'm gonna have to ask you to leave. I don't know what kind of game you're playing, but I ain't got time for the bullshit." He stood up motioning for her to leave. "Come on let's go. And yes, you do have some nice titties," he said motioning for her to leave.

"A'ight cool, I'll leave. If you don't have a problem with your wife creeping around with inmates then neither do I." Chaz got up and started towards the door.

At that moment, it all made sense. Moss computed her statement with genius like speed. "Hold on, you mean to tell me that you're Adonis Davis' wife?" he questioned with a renewed attitude.

"Duh, I thought I explained that to you," she replied before going into character. "Listen," she said while turning to face him with tears in her eyes. "I been faithful and supportive to that nigga for the last five years." She sniffled. "Then he pulls this shit," she murmured in a sob.

Moss stepped in close, pulling her into his chest. He felt her pain. "It's alright Chantell, you ain't gotta stress it." He began rubbing her back affectionately. And at the expense of her manufactured grief, his perverted ass began to catch an erection. "It's okay Chantell," he repeated as his dick swelled, pressing against her stomach. In the back of her mind, she knew she had him. "Come on now, pull it together," he spoke while rubbing her back affectionately.

Chaz sniffled then stepped away, staring at him with undeniable vulnerability showing in her face. The mere sight of her beautiful image prompted his penis to jump in his shorts. Boy did he want her. It's been months since Tonya had given him any type of pleasure, and jerking off to porn just wasn't cutting it. He needed to feel a woman's warmth, a woman's touch, and a woman's flesh.

In that moment, Chaz knew exactly what he wanted without him uttering a word. Slowly, she dropped to her knees while keeping her eyes fixed on his. Moss' breathing began to deepen as his blood boiled for her touch. Chaz grabbed the waistband of his shorts and tugged on them. Allowing them to drop down around his ankles. Just as she suspected, he had been cursed with a micro mini sausage link. She wanted to laugh her ass off at the sight of it, but she couldn't jeopardize her orders from Adonis. So with operation ninety-nine in full swing, she popped his curved, crippled looking dick into her warm, wet mouth.

Moss inhaled deeply, making a hissing sound. He was damn near on the verge of climaxing and she hadn't even begun to suck him. Steadfast, Chaz kept her eyes trained on his. Caught up in blissful excitement, he placed his hands on her head. Followed by him making the fatal mistake of leaning his head back, welcoming the moment. Then without warning, Chaz moved with the precision of a trained killer and the speed of a Mayweather jab. She dug into her sock, retrieving a straight razor just before springing to her feet. At that point murder was the only thing on her mind. Up next came the attack on his jugular. The sound of Moss' flesh ripping open was music to her ears as she cut deep into his throat.

Chaz jumped back, watching the bitch nigga grab at his neck. Though, it was useless for him to attempt such a tactic. Chaz's antagonistic smirk spread wide across her face as she witnessed his blood gush out profusely. Moss staggered a few steps forward, reaching to grab her. Yet, he fell short of getting there. He collapsed to the floor. Dieing became his fate.

Chaz kneeled down near his face. "I'm pretty sure my husband warned you that this day would come," she stated with no emotion.

Afterwards, Chaz searched the house until she found Moss' cellphone. His phone was crucial in making his murder seem like something other than what it was. After about ten minutes of searching, she found the phone upstairs on the bathroom sink. She checked to see if he had a lock on it. He didn't. "This shit is way to easy," she said before rushing back down stairs to get her phone to call Dee-Dee.

"Yeah baby, come on. I'm ready for you," Chaz told her the minute Dee-Dee answered the phone.

Within minutes, Dee-Dee was back at the house. Chaz ran outside to give her Moss phone. "Now drive to Delaware and call Tonya's phone a couple of times. Then I want you to send a few text messages to some of the people in his contacts and say, 'down in Delaware having a ball.' After that throw the phone in the Delaware River and come back so we could bury that fat bastard in the backyard."

"Why don't we just do all the texting and shit from here and then get rid of the phone. Why I gotta drive all the way to Delaware?" Dee-Dee asked, clueless of the satellite pings from cell phone towers.

"Cause once Tonya files a missing person report they gonna run his phone records and see that he was making his calls from Delaware. That way, the police will focus all their attention on Delaware instead of here," Chaz explained.

"Girl you too smart for your own good." Dee-Dee grabbed the phone. "I'll see you when I get back," she said getting back in the Buick and pulling off.

Chaz went back in the house. "I think me and Tonya gonna enjoy staying here together," she said enroute to the kitchen.

Chapter 15

Friday evening, Atlanta

Pike showed up at Flex mother's house to inform her about what New York did to her son. Which would serve as one hell of a story, because Pike had the slightest idea how he would break the news to her. Moreover, he had an obligation to do so. Even with him feeling all types of awkward, there was no way he could elude such duty.

After finding the courage to ring Sharon's bell, Pike could feel his heart pound rapidly in his chest. He hadn't seen Sharon Owens in a long time. The last time he seen her she was begging one of Flex runners to sell her a twenty piece of rock. Now here she was, about to hear that her son got his asshole rocked.

Mack Jr. could be heard trotting behind Sharon as she approached the door. The closer she got the deeper Pike's nervousness settled in. Sharon looked out the window. Instantly, she recognized her guest. In a hurry, she opened the door. She was ecstatic to see lil Pike all grown up. "Pike what a surprise," she said wholeheartedly.

Pike tried to smile and give Sharon's warm welcome the respect that it deserved, but it just wasn't working.

Sharon sensed that something was wrong. It was evident. "Come in Pike," she said waving him in as she picked Mack Jr. up before leading the way to the living room. "Have a seat and tell me what's wrong," she told Pike while taking her seat and sitting the child on her lap.

Pike didn't know where to begin. This was by far the hardest thing he had to do in his life. He tried to relax as he searched his brain for the proper way to explain what happened. Yet, that seemed virtually impossible.

"Pike just say it, tell me," Sharon begged of him.

Pike took a deep breath, "Flex got into it with his celly and he's in the hospital," he spat quickly. That was as much as he was willing to divulge. He just couldn't bring himself to tell her the exact nature of Flex's situation.

"Oh my, is he alright? What hospital is he in?" she asked with great concern. She put the baby on the couch and stood up. Frantic thoughts of her son being severely injured impeded upon her viciously. Clearly, she began to panic. "I need a hit. Pike, you got any crack on you," she blurted out.

"Ms. Owens, pull it together," Pike said standing up in an attempt to comfort her. Firmly, he hugged her. "Now you don' came too far to be going backwards. I ain't 'bout to let you relapse just because Flex done got into a little fight," he said, down playing the situation in hopes of calming her nerves. "Calm down, it ain't that serious," he stated with sympathy.

Against all of her motherly instinct, she fought to believe what he was saying to be true. Tears fell from her face. She knew Pike was holding something back. In her heart and in her mind, she just knew. So with that being said, she knew exactly who to reach out to, in order to get full disclosure of Flex's situation.

Mr. Ish

***

A few hours later

Flex laid on his stomach in the hospital heavily medicated. He was out of it. Awake, thus incoherent. His face rested on top of a medical donut as he drooled uncontrollably. He had been out of surgery for the better part of five hours and could feel nothing except the effects of the Morphine. He was handcuffed to the metal railing of the bed and under constant watch by two armed Fulton County Correctional Officers. Even though Flex had to get his rectum stitched up, no one could ignore the fact that he was still a murderous motherfucker with no regard for human life. So, it was imperative that he be guarded tightly.

Flex could hear people talking, but couldn't make out what the conversation was about. It was all mumbo jumbo to him. In fact, the guards were changing shifts. With a look of dismay, one of the reliefs approached Flex's bedside. The guard couldn't believe the type of condition he was in. It was just down right despicable that he had to endure such a monstrosity. "I'm going on a coffee run, you need something," the C.O. asked the relief at Flex bedside.

"Naw, I'm good" the guard responded. Then the doctor entered the room. "Yeah, Mr. Owens is in pretty bad shape. It'll be about two weeks before he's able to walk again. And I also placed him on a liquid diet as well." The doctor shook his head. "I'd hate for those stitches to bust open."

"Well, how many stitches did he need?" questioned the C.O. at his bedside.

"Seventy-eight altogether. Forty-four inside and thirty-four out-side. That whack job really did a number on him."

"I'm gonna get some coffee. I don't wanna hear that shit," the other C.O. replied as he left out the room.

"Let me show you where the cafeteria is," said the doctor walking out behind him.

The second that the coast was clear, Neesha whipped out her cell phone and hit Pike on speed dial. "Come on baby, you got about three minutes tops," she said quickly, then hung up. With her anxiety getting the best of her, she shuffled her keys off her belt and uncuffed Flex. About five seconds later Pike and two of his homies entered the room, scooped Flex up and put him in a wheelchair. Without delay, the two guys wheeled him out.

While Flex was being pushed casually down the corridor and out of the hospital, Pike was in the process of cuffing Neesha to the bed and relieving her of her .40 caliber. "Now remember baby, I snuck up from behind and choked you out, that's all you gotta say," explained Pike as Neesha laid on the floor in an awkward position. Then he left.

Chapter 16

3:00 am Saturday morning

Tonya slept peacefully in her bed as Chaz and Dee-Dee completed the task of digging Moss grave in the backyard. They had begun digging around seven o'clock last night and had just finished. They would have started sooner, but Dee-Dee didn't get back from Delaware until around six. And it was no way Tonya was gonna be able to help out. Her sleep deprived body just wouldn't allow it. Getting some rest was crucial for her. Anyway, the grave was dug, and it was time for Moss to be laid to rest. Thankfully, Tonya's backyard had a six-foot wooden fence around it, which gave the ladies their privacy. Unlike the ugly, grotesque dismemberment of Patty-Mae and Teesha, this was fairly clean. Not to mention, Moss had a lot of equipment stored in the garage that really helped them out. Essentially, it was as if he had prepared for this day to come.

First they used his wet vac to suck up every drop of his blood. Then they rolled his body up in the industrial tarp that he often used when painting. And once that was done, they rolled his body out of the house and down the back-patio ramp, using a couple of dollies that he would sometimes use to move heavy appliances. So yeah, the nigga definitely aided in his own burial.

Chaz stabbed the shovel into the dirt next to the flashlight. She was exhausted! Although she took countless rest and water breaks, the whole process was just a bit much. "I mean damn, you could at least help me up out of this hole," she stated while looking up at Dee-Dee.

Dee-Dee stepped to the edge of the grave. "Bitch you ain't help me when it was my turn to get up out of that hole. Standing there looking like El-Chappo tryna dig his way out of Mexico," she said laughing as she squatted down to help Chaz.

After getting Chaz back to the surface, the ladies took a seat at the patio table to discuss their future. Which was kind of foreign for them. Being as though they moved about impulsively. But times and circumstances were changing. They knew they had to have a plan as well as structure.

Chaz looked at her hands in disgust, they were filthy. "Damn! You see how trifling my hands are? Oh my goodness."

"Girl stop it. You running 'round killing everything moving and got the nerve to be complaining about dirty hands." Dee-Dee gave her a sarcastic look.

"I know right, but I'm saying though, a bitch still got class."

"I don't know about class, but you a'ight."

Chaz gave her a little smirk, "Hey, how 'bout some strawberries and wine. This is the perfect setting for a little romantic get together," she said batting her eyes.

"See what I'm saying, you ain't got no remorse about nothing. Did you forget we gotta dead Correction Officer wrapped in plastic, sitting about twenty feet from us?" Dee-Dee pointed in Moss' direction.

"Ah, yeah. But what the fuck that got to do with me wanting to share a moment with my woman." Chaz screwed her face up.

"Damn, can't a bitch have a little fun."

"Yeah Chaz, go get the strawberries and wine. You's a little spoiled bitch. Hurry up, we ain't got much time. I wanna be done with this shit before the sun come up."

Chaz jumped up and rushed off to obtain the goodies. She was always happy whenever she got her way.

"And wash those nasty ass hands," Dee-Dee added before she turned her attention to Moss' corpse. She shook her head. "I bet you was one of those C.O.'s that thought you could do whatever you wanted to do to people. Well guess what—Lieutenant Moss—everybody ain't gone just lay down to your bullshit," she said in truth as if he could really hear her. Then added, "But if ya didn't know, I bet that ass know now."

Chaz reappeared carrying a tray of chocolate covered strawberries and a cheap bottle of wine. "Here baby, we gone use these plastic cups instead of wine glasses. Gotta keep it a little hood." She giggled before filling their cups with a respectable amount of wine. "Now listen, I don't want you to touch anything. Just sit there and let me cater to you."

Dee-Dee couldn't help but blush as Chaz proceeded to feed her the strawberries. "Uhm," Dee-Dee moaned upon biting into the strawberry.

"Now don't chew or swallow. I want you to wash it down with this." Chaz took a swig of the wine as she straddled Dee-Dee and began kissing the wine into her mouth. Dee-Dee could have melted. The passion that Chaz poured into that kiss consumed them with bliss. She pulled back upon Dee-Dee swallowing. Their stare was sensual and deep. She stroked Dee-Dee's face, "I love you baby."

"I love you more," Dee-Dee replied as her heart skipped a beat. "Now be a doll and finish feeding me those Edible Arrangements."

"Edible Arrangements my ass. I dipped these myself," Chaz informed her while reaching for another strawberry.

Reasons for why she loved Chaz so much started to celebrate in her brain. It made Dee-Dee heart smile knowing that the two of them shared an unbreakable bond.

"Uhm, baby get up. Come on, let's finish this shit, I'm getting tired," Dee-Dee spoke, tapping Chaz leg for her to get up.

"Bitch you ain't tired, that's that niggaitis kicking in," Chaz replied standing up. "Come on." Chaz grabbed Dee-Dee's hand. By the time they made it to the grave, Dee-Dee could barely stand. Then she collapsed. In a flash, Chaz dropped down by her side. "Girl get up. We gotta finish this shit," she said tugging on Dee-Dee's arm. But Dee-Dee didn't respond. "Dee-Dee stop playing and get up." Still, she was unresponsive. Chaz stood up and looked down at Dee-Dee with her hands on her hips. "If you don't get up right now and stop playing I'ma leave you out here to do this shit yourself," Chaz stated in an angry whisper followed by a light kick to Dee-Dee's head. Again, Dee-Dee didn't move. Then suddenly, Chaz morphed into the killer she was born to be. Her face contoured into an angry scowl. She kneeled down, and with all her strength she pushed and pulled until she got Dee-Dee over to the grave. With Dee-Dee laying on her back and head hanging over into the hole, Chaz had the perfect angle. With all her might she jumped onto Dee-Dee's head. "Snap!" Was the sound Chaz heard. Instantly, Chaz knew she was dead.

Driven by the demons that resided within, Chaz carried on with pushing and pulling until she got Moss and Dee-Dee bodies in the grave. "Finally," she exclaimed, looking down in the grave. "And if yo ass wasn't so greedy it wouldn't have been so easy to get rid of yo ass," Chaz said in reference to the Xanax spiked strawberries she fed Dee-Dee. "But." Chaz grabbed the shovel and scooped up some dirt, "I'll always love you," she said before tossing the dirt onto Dee-Dee's face.

"Girl you still out here," Tonya said from the patio.

Chaz turned around, "Uh, yeah. This shit ain't as simple as it seems. Now that you all rested and shit, you could come down here and help a bitch out."

"A'ight, let me throw on some clothes."

***

About ten minutes later Tonya was back. "So now what?" Tonya asked, making her way down the patio steps.

"Now nothing." Chaz shrugged her shoulders. "We bury these two assholes and focus on getting Adonis home."

A smile of delight graced Tonya's face. Hearing the words Adonis and home in the same sentence warmed her heart. "That's what's up." Tonya grabbed the other shovel. "Wow, is that Dee-Dee?" she asked, not realizing that Chaz spoke of burying two people.

Without a smidgen of remorse, Chaz answered. "Yeah, that's her." Chaz put the shovel down and closed in on Tonya. "Look Tonya, I love my brother with all my heart. He's all I have. Even though I love Dee-Dee, she had to go. I couldn't risk her tryna do something to you. She was talking crazy. Trust me, she had to go." Chaz gave her a false look of concern before picking the shovel backup to pack in the dirt.

Tonya had never felt so safe and secure in her life. She just knew she found herself the best sister-in-law this cruel world had to offer. She wasn't even concerned that Chaz was a stone-cold killer. As long as her safety, and the safety of her child wasn't compromised, she was all in. "Yeah lets get this shit done," she expressed warmly then grabbed the other shovel.

The sun had just started to creep over the horizon as the ladies finished filling the grave. Even though there were still a few things that Chaz needed to do, she had accomplished what she needed for the time being. "A'ight girl, that's it for now." Chaz tossed her shovel to the side. "I'm tired, dirty and hungry. So if you'll excuse me, I got normal people shit to do," said Chaz, advertising her level of exhaustion.

"Seed planted, go ahead and handle your business. I'll clean this mess up and put everything away. As far as I'm concerned, this is your house too." Tonya smiled.

Chaz gave her one of those —I'm so grateful for your hospitality—looks. But thought to herself, bitch I don't need your approval to do shit.

When Chaz got upstairs to the bathroom she damn near lost her mind. Seeing a bloody tampon in the waist basket pushed her to entertain a few questionable thoughts. "I hope this bitch can explain this shit!" Chaz exclaimed while unraveling some toilet tissue to grab the bloody tampon out of the garbage. "If this bitch ain't pregnant I'ma kill her ass," she grunted as she made her way downstairs. Just as she reached the bottom of the stairs, Tonya rounded the corner.

"Tonya, what the hell is this?" Chaz questioned with anger while holding the tampon up for Tonya to see.

Shocked, and totally caught off guard, Tonya's face went blank. Her heart began racing and fear of what Chaz might do next struck her to the core. She didn't know what to do.

"Bitch, you better tell me something! 'Cause I'm 'bout to make that ass disappear!"

Tonya's mouth twitched nervously, "I, uh, well."

"Spit it out bitch, you better tell me something!" Chaz snapped in a rage.

"It's fake!" Tonya blurted out.

Chaz exhaled in frustration, "I'ma count to three and if you don't tell me what the fuck is going on, you and your husband gonna be discussing y'all differences when you get to hell."

Tears attacked Tonya's eyes without prejudice. In a broken murmur she spoke, "I use that to keep my husband from asking for sex," she cried.

Chaz balled her face up. She looked at the tampon with disdain before busting out laughing. "Oh that's a good one. I ain't think about that," she stated with a giggle before stepping off.

Tonya stood in the hallway teetering on the verge of a breakdown. She wasn't stable in the least. Slowly, she wiped away the tears and gathered herself the best she could. Just then, Chaz called out for her to come upstairs. Without thought, Tonya was on her way.

"Knock, knock." Tonya tapped on the bathroom door.

"Come in," Chaz invited.

Tonya entered. Automatically, her level of jealousy and envy shot to great heights. She felt insecure. Oh my god, this heffa body is tighter than a virgin pussy, she thought while taking notice of how beautiful Chaz's body was. "Yeah, what's up?" Tonya asked as her eyes drifted the length of the specimen before her.

Chaz turned around, ready to step in the shower. "Can you give me something to wear until we go get my stuff from Jersey City." She stepped one foot in the shower and turned back to face Tonya. "I hope I am not inconveniencing you?" she said smiling.

Tonya's world went blank as she began screaming inside her head. *Inconvenience! Bitch is you serious? First you come up in my house and kill my husband. Then you killed your girlfriend. Buried them in my backyard. And to make matters worse, you just threatened to kill me like ten minutes ago. Inconvenience, are you fucking kidding me?!—* "Of course not, the last thing you need to worry about is something like that. We family now, and family gotta stick together," she stated after interrupting her thoughts.

"Thanks girl, you are just full of hospitality," Chaz concluded before committing to her shower.

"Don't mention it," Tonya replied with a snarling smirk as she left.

Chapter 17

7:02 am, same morning

Down in Atlanta

The Captain stood on the other side of the two way mirror—of the interrogation room— watching on as Erica drilled Neesha. Every question that Erica asked seemed to hold a harsh over tone. Getting to the bottom of Flex's escape became her current passion. Despite their relationship and love for one another, Erica wasn't about to invoke any type of favoritism. Especially with her superior scrutinizing the interview.

"Now I'm pretty sure your story ain't gonna change being as though we went over this about a thousand times," Erica said pacing back and forth.

Neesha rolled her eyes, "Well if you know my story ain't gonna change, why the fuck you keep asking me the same shit over and over again!"

Erica's hand came crashing down on the table. Boom! She got up in Neesha's breathing space, "Because I'm asking the fucking questions, that's why!" she responded viciously.

Neesha was taken aback. There started to be an unsettling tantrum rising within her. Somehow though, she managed to control herself. "Look detective, like I said a million times, my partner and the doctor went for coffee. As I went to pull up a chair next to Mr. Owens, somebody came from behind and choked me out," she explained in a cool-tempered tone.

Mikros entered the interrogation room, "Detective, I need a minute."

Erica shot Neesha a narrowed eye stare before stepping out the room with Mikros. "What, what is it Mikros?" she asked closing the door behind them while simultaneously pulling the scrunchy off of her ponytail.

"There seems to be a lot more going on involving Mr. Owens' case than we initially knew about." Mikros held up a folder.

Erica grabbed it, "What are you talking about?" she said opening the folder.

"That's a joint report from our coroner's office and the Maryland State Police. Its been determined that one of the victims that we discovered inside Mr. Owens' trunk is from New Jersey. DNA pegs victim number one as Patty-Mae Mason of Jersey City, New Jersey."

Erica didn't know what the hell was going on. She listened to what Mikros was saying, but still couldn't quite get what the connection was.

"But here's the kicker," Mikros continued, "I went over the surveillance tapes from The Ivy and the night before we received the anonymous tip." Mikros stopped to catch his breath. "There was a blue Buick Regal with New Jersey plates parked next to Mr. Owens' Lexus."

Erica looked up at him perplexed. Her lack of insight on the case encouraged her expression.

Mikros continued, "So whoever was driving the Buick is the person responsible for the butchered bodies found in the Lexus."

Erica closed the folder, "And how do you know that?"

"Well…because that's the tale of the tape." Mikros smiled.

"So, you mean to tell me Michael Owens was set up?"

"That's exactly what the fuck I'm telling you!" he punctuated.

"Well do we know who the Buick belongs to?" she asked.

"Okay are you ready for this?" he asked excitedly.

"Cut the shit and tell me!" Erica snapped.

Mikros rolled his eyes. "The Buick is registered to the deceased, Patty-Mae Mason."

"A'ight Mikros." Erica shook her head with utter surprise. "Let me wrap this interview up and I'll catch up with you in a minute. Did you go over the security tapes from the hospital?"

"That's where the curve ball comes in at. Apparently, the cameras weren't working at the time. The Chief of the security company is looking into it. He's willing to help out as much as possible."

Erica didn't care to comment. She just handed him back the folder and re-entered the interrogation room. "Okay Ms. Wallace, you're free to go. If we need any further information I'll contact you personally," Erica said with a bit of an attitude.

"Oh please, save yourself the trouble and call my union rep. Better yet, call my lawyer!" Neesha said hastily as she got up from the table.

"Do yourself a favor Ms. Wallace, don't leave the state," Erica remarked.

"Kiss my ass!" Neesha shouted as she stormed out.

***

The Captain ordered Mikros and Erica to accompany him in the Commissioner's office. He be damned if he got chewed out by his lonesome. Its been less than twenty-four hours since Flex's escape—and as it stood—nobody had a clue on where to start. Shame faced, the trio filed in to see the Commissioner, who was on the phone with the Mayor.

The Commissioner pulled the receiver away from his mouth and covered it. "Shut the fucking door!" he screamed in a whisper before getting back to his call. "Yes, yes sir. Sure thing," he said to the

Mayor then hung up.

The Commissioner took a slow deep breath. "Listen Sam," he said to the Captain. "As bad as this situation is." He paused and took another deep breath, then exhaled. "I'm gonna do something that could possibly get me fired at best. But, I don't give a squirrel's dick about any of that!" He pointed a stern finger at the Captain. "Now before any of this leaks out, and the media decides to crucify the department. I want you to find this son-of-a-bitch, and I want his ass. Dead or alive! Do I make myself clear?" the Commissioner growled with vicious anger.

"Yes sir, quite clear sir," the Captain responded with hopes of being dismissed. At this point, all he wanted to do was get out of the Commissioners sight. He hated being talked down to. Especially in the company of his detectives.

"Now before I let you all go, I got the Georgia Bureau of Investigations and the FBI crawling up the Mayor's ass. They're itching to take this case from us." The Commissioner began pointing again, "But I'm willing to put my ass in a sling to protect the integrity of this department." He sighed a—please lord help me—sigh, then continued. "You got"... He looked at his watch. "Forty-seven hours to find Mr. Owens, starting in twelve minutes. You're all dismissed," the Commissioner stated waving them out.

After leaving the Commissioner's office, Erica couldn't help but feel the need to take charge. From what she'd seen so far, there could be no way she'd feel comfortable with letting the Captain run the show, let alone Mikros. Although she was the last person on the totem pole in terms of seniority, she'd be a dikes nipple before playing the back seat in this situation. Especially with Mikros' track record of half assing his investigations. After all, her livelihood depended on it.

When they got to the Captain's office, Erica transformed like never before. It was as if crossing the Captain's threshold ignited the unforeseen monster/beast that lay dormant inside her small, yet beautiful body. Her eyes grew cold with darkness and her face shifted into that of an angry bitch on a mission.

"Listen up!" Erica stated in a demanding voice. "Please don't take this the wrong way." She turned and shut the door. "Obviously, you crackers don't know what the fuck y'all doing, how to go about doing it, or where to start at!"

Mikros and the Captain looked at each other like, who the fuck does this nigger bitch think she is.

"Now have a seat and let me explain a few things," she roared, imposing herself authoritatively.

The gentlemen obliged more out of disbelief than for any other reason.

Erica walked around the Captain's desk and stood in front of them. There was a slight moment of silence on her behalf. Then she got right to it. "Mikros, I want you to put pressure on everybody that's associated with Michael Owens. I don't care if you gotta offer them money, drugs or some dick. Do whatever you gotta do to collect as many leads as possible." Next, she turned her attention to her superior. "Captain, I need you to pull back on having Mr. Owens' mother tailed. The last thing he is gonna do is jeopardize his mom. Black people don't do shit like that. It's a waste of manpower. Also, I'ma need you to contact the Jersey City Police Department and have them sit on Ms. Mason's residence. If anything illegal is going on there, call in a favor and have them turn a blind eye. It makes perfect sense that Mr. Owens could possibly be making a stop at that location. We don't need to compromise our operation." Erica unholstered her .40 caliber, checked the clip then stated, "Also make it clear that Mr. Owens is armed and extremely dangerous," she concluded while reholstering her gun.

Bright eyed and excited the Captain chimed in. "What a fucking impressive strategy. You wanna give Mr. Owens the leverage to move about freely in hopes that he shows himself," the Captain expressed as if he figured it all out.

Erica crinkled her nose, "Uh no. That's not the plan at all. The plan is to make it appear that we're doing everything we can to find Mr. Owens. But when our forty-seven hours expire, I'll be all for handing this case over to another agency. 'Cause to tell you the truth Captain, I'm tired of this crazy ass case!"

"Amen to that sister," Mikros shouted, raising a clenched fist.

The Captain looked at Erica with confusion. He didn't know how to take her proposal. It sounded to him like she was purposely trying to botch the investigation. Which was something he had never seen. Never in all his years on the force, had he heard of an underling having the brazen audacity to tell a superior that they wanted to literally fuck up on an investigation. Let alone, the capture of an escaped serial killer and pyromaniac. But to be honest, the Captain was all for it. Because the last thing the Captain wanted to do was to invest anymore energy into trying to catch Michael 'Flex' Owens. It was just too much. So for the moment, Erica's lazy, unethical and sideways method of public service was in direct accordance with what the Captain's heart truly desired.

"Well first of all," the Captain finally broke his silence. "If we're gonna take a back seat to doing our jobs and give up on our sworn duties, then we're gonna have to bare some thick skin for the backlash that's to follow." The Captain exhaled, "Now I'm not exactly sure how it's gonna play out, but we gotta keep this our little secret." He stood up. "As long as we show that we made some type of effort then we'll be good." The Captain waved his hand, "Now get the hell back to work!" he smiled deviously.

***

After arriving at their desk, Erica jumped right into handling her business.

"Mikros, make me a copy of everything you've received from the Maryland State Police. And get me a copy of that statement Mr. Owens made to Wiggins about the girl Chaz. I gotta hunch that I need to follow," Erica explained as she gathered some papers from her cubicle.

"What's up, you need me to tag along?"

"Naw, it's nothing really. I just need to cross check a few things that's all. I'll give you a call in about an hour. Come on now, go make me those copies. I gotta go."

When Mikros returned, Erica grabbed the papers from him and got on her way. She couldn't wait around for a bunch of nothing to transpire. She needed to at least put forth an empty effort so she could keep her job. A slick tactic that she picked up from the late Detective Kliens. Only difference was, she intended on making her fake attempts at public service count for more than most could imagine.

***

11:34 am,
Fulton County Jail

Ironically, Adonis had been placed in Flex's old cell. And still, the stench of booty musk still lingered in the air. It was a stale yet noticeable scent, despite the cleaning that the trustees gave. Nevertheless, Adonis hadn't left the cell since he arrived yesterday afternoon. He ate lunch when he first got there, showered and slept through dinner and breakfast. Now here it was, lunch time again.

Adonis was in the process of washing up at the sink when his cell door slid open. The abrupt sound hampered his movement for a moment. He tossed his wash rag in the sink and stepped to the opening. Shirtless, he peeked his head out to quickly assess the reason his cell door had opened. Mess out, he said in his head just before the C.O. yelled it out. At that point inmates began coming out of their cells. On their way to the chow line a few inmates with curious eyes gazed over at Adonis, gawking at the giant man whose physical stature intimidated the average Joe. There was no denying how monstrous Adonis looked with super hero-like muscles tailored to his physique.

Adonis took a few more seconds to survey the tier before grabbing his shirt for Mess. After getting his tray he returned to his cell. He wasn't beat for conversation. Nor was he trying to give up the intimidation factor that his silence evoked.

Adonis folded the mat back on the top bunk, using the metal platform to serve as his table. As he stood there eating, South Woods State Prison whizzed into his head. He smiled as Tonya's face popped up out of nowhere. Then he suddenly stopped eating. That garbage ass meal did nothing for him. He couldn't believe that the state of Georgia approved of such bullshit to be fed to inmates.

Adonis looked at the tray and laughed. He was slightly amused by his overall situation. For some reason it tickled him. "All I need is a chance. Just one chance to touch them streets," he said in his head. Adonis grabbed the bread off the tray, it was the only thing worth consuming. Just as he washed it down with a cup of water, his cell door was opening again. The call for trays to be returned rang out. Still, Adonis didn't bother to break his silence as he dumped his tray. Yet, the eyes of what seemed like the whole tier were on him.

"Davis!" yelled the C.O. "You gotta visit."

Adonis cut the walk to his cell short and headed towards the officers' booth. Visit! He thought in stride to meet with the guard. "I'ma kick her ass," he said to the open air, assuming it was Chaz that came to see him. Moreover, when he got to the officers' booth, the C.O. informed him that he had a consultation as opposed to a civilian visit. Immediately, he figured it was a public defender. Although he wasn't due in court until Monday, the timing was perfect in terms of an update. A greasy grin graced his lips. "This motherfucker better give me some type of good news, "he told himself while waiting for the unit door to open.

When Adonis got to the consultation room, he shook his head in annoyance at the sight of Erica sitting there. He could have sworn that he made it clear to her that they had nothing to discuss. Now here she was, showing up at the jail. As if something was gonna change.

"I ain't got nothing to say to you. If you have questions speak to my lawyer," Adonis snapped as soon as he entered the room.

"Mr. Davis, you're in no position to reject this little get together I've constructed," Erica said then smiled sharply. "Now sit yo ass down!" she barked before changing her tone. "Besides, Chaz—I mean Chantell's life depends on it," she said in a sarcastically yet threatening tone.

Erica was now talking his language. There was nothing in the world that could capture Adonis' attention the way a threat on Chaz's life could. With a burning rage to break Erica's neck stirring inside of him, he was even surprised that he didn't react. "I love you Adonis," echoed in his head as Chaz's voice spoke to him out of nowhere.

"Aww, ain't that sweet. You're standing there like you ready to fuck me up. Well... I would strongly advise you to think long and hard about that. I'm pretty sure you're smarter than that," Erica said.

Adonis wanted so badly to react, but he couldn't. Chaz was too delicate for him to jeopardize. Slowly, he relaxed. Followed by a sigh. But that sigh wasn't a sigh of defeat, rather it expressed compromise. Because that's exactly what he intended on doing for the moment—compromise! "You know what, I don't know what kind of bullshit you tryna pull, but whatever. I'ma play along for now, but if anything happens to—

"Oh please!" Erica stood up, tossing all professionalism out the window. "I think you need to sit the fuck down and listen to what the hell I'm 'bout to tell you."

"Yo..." Adonis pointed, amped with aggression. "You got me fucked up. I ain't none of these pooh-putt ass Atlanta niggas," he stated with his nostrils flared.

Erica loved every minute of the power she possessed. She was now the one in control and Adonis knew it. What a turn around. He was no longer the self-absorbed, cocky dude she had extradited from

New Jersey. Naw, that nigga musta disappeared. Because as it stood, it was Erica's turn to exhibit arrogance.

Finally, Adonis took a seat. He was heated.

Erica placed her hands flat on the table across from where he sat. "Now do I have to call for restraints while we talk about this?" Her words were much calmer.

"Naw, I'm good. Come on, let me hear what you got to say." Adonis sat back and crossed his arms.

Erica's mouth embodied a devilish grin. Got 'em, she thought before sitting back down. "Ok, here's the deal. First and foremost, tell me how you know Tyrone?"

Adonis gave her a wrinkled brow stare, "What is it with you and Tyrone. Why you so pressed for my help?"

"Listen Mr. Davis, speaking on a personal note and all things serious, that nigga Tyrone is the worst of the worst. He is so twisted and sick that I often ask God how could he allow someone like that to be created." Erica paused and began fingering through the files she brought with her. A deep sigh of anger escaped her as she retrieved New York's file, pulling out his rape case. "Here, take a look at these photos." She slid them across the table.

Just the mere sight of the abused child motivated Adonis to cringe, he slid them back. "I can't look at those. I already know what type of shit that weirdo is into."

"Look, I'ma be straightforward with you. If you could take care of this situation, permanently! Then you will have no problem with getting your case dismissed."

A sly chuckle escaped him, "Now you gonna sit up here and tell me that you got the power to get my case tossed." He was too amused. There was no way in hell that he would ever believe that Erica had the power to get his case thrown out.

"It's not about power, it's about intelligence. Believe me Mr. Davis, intelligence is what my career is predicated on." she expressed hubrisly.

"Before we discuss anything further, I'm gonna need confirmation that Chaz is safe and that no harm will come her way."

Erica got up and knocked on the window, grabbing the guard's attention. "Can you bring me a phone? I need an outside line." Her request wasn't questioned. Within a minute the C.O. was bringing her the phone.

"Here you go ma'am," said the guard handing her the phone.

"Thank you," she replied ever so politely.

"You something else you know that," Adonis said the minute Erica shut the door.

She giggled. "Here, call whoever you gotta call and you'll see that Chaz is safe. But listen," she gave him a—but wait, there's more—look. "You need to let her know that she has to get rid of that Buick and she can't stay at that Ocean Avenue address in Jersey City."

Inquisitively, Adonis' face transformed. "Where is all of this coming from," he asked, wondering if she was trying to pull a fast one to somehow get confirmation on Chaz whereabouts.

Erica released the phone, then walked around to her side of the table. "Ok, here's the deal." she said sitting down and separating the files she had stacked in a pile.

Adonis had the slightest idea about what her pretty ass was in the process of doing. But whatever it was, it had better been good, 'cause the more he thought about her trying to play him, the more he was inclined to snap her fucking neck.

"Let's start with you." Erica grabbed the folder marked Adonis Davis. She opened it and pulled out the reports. "In the summer of 2000, you shot and killed a teenage boy in front of a liquor store. His name was Travis Owens." She sat that folder to the side then grabbed another one. "Now fast forward fifteen years later. Your adopted sister, Chantell, aka Chaz had become our lead suspect in connection with a series of murders and arsons." Erica grabbed another folder. "And coincidentally Michael Owens, who happens to be the brother of the kid you killed, gave this undocumented statement." She slid the statement to Adonis. "Implicating Chantell and some other females as the ones responsible."

"But Chantell is in the clear now," Adonis interjected as he looked down at the undocumented statement that Flex gave the late Detective Wiggins.

"True, but not exactly. We had cleared Chantell because all of the evidence seemed to point back to Michael." Erica rushed to grab a different file. "Until this newly discovered information surfaced," she said sliding him more documents and pictures.

Adonis took a few moments to go over the papers, wondering what any of this had to do with Chaz. That is until he came across the name Patty-Mae Mason being among the deceased. Qua's mom, he thought as his blood pressure rose. His head began to spin. How in the world could this be possible? he thought. Then he flicked through the still cropped photos from The Ivy surveillance footage that clearly showed Dee-Dee putting large plastic bags inside of Flex's trunk. But after a more thorough observation of the information before him, he knew that Chaz was the one responsible. There was no denying it. It reeked of her doing through and through.

Adonis leaned back in his chair burying his face in his hands. "A'ight," he said, exhaling and removing his hands. "A'ight, so where we at with all of this? What exactly is it that you need me to do?"

Erica's face lit up. That was all she needed to hear. "Well listen, as it stands no one in my department knows the facts to this extent except me. Now what I can do is see to it that Chaz stay in the clear. And I'll pull some strings to have your bail reduced low enough so you could bail out."

He had no way of knowing if the bitch was pulling his leg or not, but what she was talking was sounding real good. Good to the point that his dick began to swell.

Adonis put his fist up to his forehead, tapping it lightly.

"Listen Adonis, go ahead and make your call to Chaz. Now remember, tell her to stay away from that Ocean Avenue address until she hears back from you." Erica's tone was soothing and subtle. It was almost as if she could be trusted. However, Adonis wasn't the type to embrace people so easily. Either way, he had nothing to lose and everything to gain. He jogged his memory for Tonya's number, then made the call.

Chapter 18

1:57 pm

Tony's house

Bridgeton, New Jersey

It was nearing two in the afternoon as Tonya was just finishing up with getting most of Moss' belongings into the cab of his truck. She intended on driving it over to North Philly and leaving it for the crackheads to dispose of. Which was actually a smart idea. Then her phone rung.

Tonya put the suitcase down and answered the call. Her eyes smiled the instant she heard Adonis' voice.

"Hello," he said with the quickness.

"Oh my goodness, hey baby. Are you alright?" she asked excitedly yet concerned.

"Yeah I'm good but listen, I'ma need you to go to my sister's house and—

"Baby Chaz over here at my house," Tonya explained cutting him off.

"A'ight cool, put her on the phone." He pierced at Erica trying to get a read on her.

"Hold on baby," Tonya said waking Chaz up. "Here Chaz take the phone. It's your brother."

"Uhm," Chaz moaned as she stretched out to grab the phone. Lethargically, she sat up. It was obvious that she was still exhausted. "Yeah baby," she said in a groggy voice, not realizing her slip of the tongue.

"Hey wake up. I need you to be on point with what I'm 'bout to tell you."

"Uhm okay. I'm up. I'm up." She gathered herself.

"A'ight look, I just found out that some nigga named Michael Owens killed my man Qua's mom. Her name was Patty-Mae. I need you to stay where you at until I figure out what the hell is going on. I go to court on Monday and hopefully I'll get a bail that I could post," Adonis explained, making sure he pinned Flex as Patty-Mae's killer in case the phone call was being recorded.

"I got you. I had planned on doing that anyway. Your wife needs all the help she could get," Chaz said cutting her eyes at Tonya, giving her a big smile. "Oh, and I solved those ninety-nine problems too. Now are you sure you don't need me to come down there?" Chaz stood up, computing that more was at stake than Adonis alluded to. Racing thoughts invaded her mind.

"Naw, don't leave that house until I give you the green light. It's a lot going on right now and I gotta figure this shit out."

"A'ight I got you. But you need to explain those arrangements to Tonya, hold on." Chaz handed Tonya the phone and went to the bathroom.

"Yeah, I'm here," spoke Tonya.

"Look baby, I don't want Chaz leaving that house so make sure you keep her ass indoors until you hear otherwise." The authority in his voice put her on edge.

"What happened baby, is everything alright?"

"Yeah, everything good. And hopefully by the end of this week I should be home, that is if everything goes right."

Erica winked at him.

"Adonis, whatever you need me to do I'ma do. I love you." Tonya's words were sincere.

"I love you too," he replied casually.

"Oh, and I almost forgot. Quaheem Mason gave me that message," Tonya stated.

"Message, what message?" He asked, unsure of what Qua was up to.

"I mean basically he was just telling me what you told him to tell me." Tonya explained to him.

"Oh yeah. Yeah, he's good people baby. But dig, it's a lot going on right now and I ain't got time to explain. Just stay clear of Qua for now." Adonis computed that Qua must have been trying to work an angle of his own, which he had no problem with. But at the same time, he didn't want Tonya being the recipient of collateral damage if Qua found out that Chaz was involved in his mother's murder. Assuming that Qua already knew that his mother had been killed.

"Well I put some money in your account. And don't be in there stressing, we gone get through this," Tonya expressed. The last part of her comment dripped with uncertainty. Though she prayed that she spoke the truth.

"A'ight baby, I gotta go. I'll call you later." Adonis said before hanging up, totally forgetting to mention the Buick. "So, now what's the next step?" he questioned Erica with a hint of attitude.

"Its simple, I just have to put things in motion so you can handle your end of the deal and then we'll take it from there," she expressed without feelings.

"Hold the fuck up, I ain't 'bout ta body that nigga in here. For all I know you could be playing me and I'd never get the fuck out. If you wanna make this deal go through, you need to figure out a way for me and Ty-dog to meet up on the streets."

Erica's eyes grew big at the mention of the name Ty-dog. "Mr. Davis," she spoke calmly. "What exactly is the nature of you and Tyrone's association?"

"It ain't no association between me and him. Don't think for one second that me and that foul ass nigga cool." Adonis anger was once again on the rise.

"There has to be more than what you're telling me. Because the only people that know Tyrone Newsome as Ty-dog, is family and those he grew up with. Being as though there's a big age gap between y'all, I'm inclined to believe there's something you're not telling me."

"I believe there's something you're not telling me," Adonis repeated sarcastically. "Listen bitch," he began talking with his hands. "You think you got it all figured out don't you. Well let me tell you something. You have the slightest idea about that nigga Tyrone. I been wanting to get at that nigga. Just the thought of making that nigga suffer for hours before killing him makes my dick hard."

"Oh, so you wanna fuck'em," she joked.

Adonis slammed his fist down hard on the table, "He raped my wife you silly bitch!" Adonis roared with intensity.

"Are you alright ma'am?" asked the C.O. after barging in at the sound of Adonis abrupt rant.

"I'm fine." Erica dismissed the guard with a wave of the hand. "Wife?... What are you talking about Mr. Davis?" she asked confused.

Adonis took a deep breath and sat back. "Chaz isn't just my adopted sister, she's my wife."

Erica's mouth gaped open in surprise. That was the last thing she was expecting to hear. Her outlook on the whole situation had just evolved. "So, you're telling me that Chaz is your wife? How long have you two been married?" This stunning revelation afforded her the opportunity to gain an amended perspective.

There was a slow response on Adonis part. He took a calming breath. "When my mother first adopted Chaz it took her a while to open up about the things that went on with her. Chaz was dealing with a lot of issues and she didn't trust nobody." Adonis looked away, it pained him to tell this story. "But eventually, Chaz came around to confiding in me." Tears began to well in his eyes. He sniffled. "And when she told me what her uncle Tyrone had done to her. I promised her I'd never let that sick bastard hurt her ever again. Him or anyone else." Adonis was now giving Erica an evil stare.

Erica's heart sank as she witnessed the emotional breakdown of the man who sat before her. The sympathy she felt for Chaz moved her in a way that couldn't be explained. It was no way that she was gonna leave Adonis out to dry. How could she, knowing what she knows now? "Mr. Davis, you don't have to second guess what I told you. But just to reassure that my word is my bond, I'm gonna see to it that all evidence that implicates Chantell never has the chance at being admitted into our records. Chantell is clear and free, but to secure your spot as a free man, you're gonna have to oblige my initial proposal."

"Look detective."

"Erica, just call me Erica," she interrupted.

"A'ight Erica," he said, prior to leaning forward. It was obvious that he felt more comfortable. "Don't you think it's best to kill this nigga outside the jail? I'm saying, don't that give us a lot more leverage to dispose of the body?"

"I agree all the way, but there isn't any way for me to get Tyrone released. No judge or prosecutor is gonna agree to any type of relief for him. Especially after that horrendous ordeal with Michael Owens."

Adonis' face tightened, "What happened between them?"

Erica tried to compose herself, but she couldn't. A high-pitched laugh shot from her mouth. She began crying from laughter. It was crazy.

"What, what's so funny?" Adonis questioned just before laughing himself.

Although Erica's actions were inappropriate by all accounts, she for some reason found humor in the fact that Flex got his asshole ripped open.

Erica fought to control herself. Thankfully she was able to do so. Otherwise, she would have surely obsessed about her moral defect later on. "That sick bastard sodomized Mr. Owens," she stated with disdain.

"You mean like fucked him in his butt?" Adonis questioned with a twisted face.

"That's exactly what I mean," Erica reiterated flatly.

"Shit, that's on him." Adonis shrugged his shoulders. "I mean it's fucked up but at the same time fuck both them niggas. If I had it my way I'd bury 'em both in the same box."

"I hear you, but now you see why it'll be impossible to get Tyrone's bail lowered."

There was a pause between them. "A'ight here's the deal. I'll take care of Tyrone after my arraignment on Monday, but you gotta throw in that nigga Michael as an incentive. I can't let that joker live knowing he's the one that basically put Chaz in this situation."

Erica stood up extending her hand. "You have yourself a deal." She smiled, neglecting to tell Adonis that Flex had escaped.

Chapter 19

Saturday, 6:17 pm Atlanta

"Ohh, yeah. Fuck me, fuck me harder," the bitch whined. Obligingly, he pounded with a bit more force. The sloppy sounds of their bodies being involved in such an episode infected the atmosphere of the small area they occupied. Luckily, there was no one around to investigate or witness what was taking place. He could feel the pulp of the bitch insides secrete. Saturating his dick with butt butter as he gyrated his hips. Mumbles and moans of pleasure spewed from them both as their ratchet, sexual indulgence continued to flare. Its been a while since they've had the chance to creep, credited to all the drama going on in Atlanta.

"It's happening, ohh, it's happening," he called out at the point of climax. Mikros could feel the Captain's legs buckle as he got weak in the knees. Mikros loved it when the Captain reacted like that when busting off inside of him. Reinforcing in Mikros' head that he had some top-notch boy pussy.

Element of Surprise II

After the Captain withdrew his shitty dick from Mikros and wiped himself clean, the two went back to being officers of the law. "Grab that Febreze over there and spray down this room before you leave," instructed the Captain as he left out. He didn't even give Mikros a chance to rid himself of the oozing semen from his butt before making his departure. Leaving Mikros feeling like a side bitch, abandoned by her married boyfriend. Nevertheless, satisfied.

Ironically, Erica and the Captain met up at his office at the same time, both having made progress—if you wanna call it that.

"So yeah, I got Mikros doing a little damage control on a personal matter. Now what's the deal with what you got going on?" inquired the Captain as they took a seat in his office.

Erica wasn't stupid, she knew them crackers had been fucking for months. That lil dirty secret though, was the furthest thing from her mind. Given the fact that her brain was currently being occupied by what her and Adonis agreed on. Because at that point she didn't give a fuck about Flex's case. "You know, same ole same ole. Just waiting for our time to expire so we could rid ourselves of this headache that Mr. Owens seem to bring everyone," Erica divulged comfortably.

"Glad to know we're on the same page. Now, Mikros said something about the surveillance footage from The Ivy and a Buick. What's that about?" the Captain questioned.

Erica shook her head slightly at the question, thinking to herself how loose Mikros lips were even when he wasn't sucking dick. "Actually, it's like a big deal. But I'm not gonna tell you. That way, when or if the shit hits the fan you're protected. The last thing I wanna do is compromise your career and give Michael Owens a loophole to wiggle himself out of." She explained then gave the Captain a devious look.

And of course the Captain reframed from prying any further. If nothing else, he didn't give a shit either way. As far as his racist, gay ass was concerned, all niggers and their children could die. Just don't fuck with his pension.

"I always knew there was something wonderful about you," the Captain replied with a shitty grin then continued. "Would it be too much of a stretch to ask you to prepare all files and evidence to be turned over to the GBI for Monday. Minus the full disclosure of whatever it is you feel they don't need to know."

Just as Erica was about to answer Mikros knocked on the door. Upon him entering the office, the faint scent of the Captain's after-shave could be smelled on him.

"Disgusting motherfuckers," Erica blurted out unexpectedly.

"Excuse me," said the Captain.

"Nothing Captain. My mind just wandered a bit," Erica remarked.

"Okay," said the Captain before changing gears. "Let's look at where we are and what needs to be done moving forward."

Mikros picked up, "We're exactly where we were prior to this briefing. Mr. Owens is still missing, none of us gives a fuck and we're just wasting time until Monday."

"No argument there, but for the sake of keeping our jobs we gotta stay on point with our..." The Captain paused slightly then made air quotation marks, "concerted efforts," he explained.

"Like I said before, as long as we have a trail of what seems like transparency in trying to recapture Mr. Owens, there shouldn't be anything to worry about," Erica said re-establishing her position on the matter.

Mikros threw his hands up as if to say—fuck it, let this bitch run the Michael Owens circus.

"Alright then, I see no need in bumping our gums any longer. I'll see you both tomorrow. Oh and try to get here early, despite the weekend. Because on Monday, I'm expecting a visit from the Commissioner and the rest of his ball licking crew," the Captain stated while giving them a dismissive hand gesture.

***

Once cleared of the Captain's presence, Mikros had a few things he wanted to express to Erica in terms of the whole Flex situation.

Not to mention, he also wanted to give her a piece of his mind in regard to how she chose to run things. Actually, the cracker felt a little salty that she had some underhand shit going on without including him. He knew because it was obvious that the bitch was on some shady shit. And as her partner, he felt alienated.

Erica plopped down in her chair, retrieving the vibrating phone from her hip. She read the text then sat the phone down on her desk. Just then Mikros approached, "Okay, so here's the deal. There are a number of things that we need to chat about, but nothing too serious."

Erica gazed with unwavering eyes, casting a— 'so what the fuck we gotta talk about?'— stare.

"By all means, speak your peace," she enlightened him.

"Let me just start by saying you are one hell of a difficult woman to figure out. At first, I couldn't seem to put the pieces together, but I got it now." Mikros pulled up a seat and almost fell when he went to sit down. "I am so clumsy at times," he said catching himself and taking his seat. "So, look here Miss Sneaky and Secretive. We're partners, despite how you feel about me on a personal level. I'm the one person you can count on to have your back through any and everything. Now if you'd be so kind as to tell me who the father is, I promise I won't judge you."

"Father of who and what the hell are you talking about?" she questioned, oblivious to what the hell Mikros was talking about.

"Really, you gone sit up here and play that role with me? Girl you need to stop. Everybody could see that you've gained weight. It's showing everywhere." Mikros moved his hands awkwardly in the air as he explained himself. "Girl your face done got fat, your hips are spreading and not to mention your attitude has been awful towards everybody."

"Wow, you really are the world's dumbest detective. No stupid, I'm not pregnant and if I was, what the fuck does that have to do with you? In case you forgot, you're gay Mikros. The only thing you should be focused on is the damage control issues the Captain be sending you on, not investigating my personal business," she expressed lividly.

There was a slight moment of silence as Mikros gaped at her with evil eyes. Then he busted out laughing. "Bitch let me find out you mad 'cause I get more dick than you."

"Boy please, I ain't got time for this shit. I'll see you in the morning. And when you get a chance, dispose of all information about that Buick and those tapes from The Ivy. We don't need the alphabet boys hanging around any longer than they need to, and believe me, that newly discovered intel would definitely keep them doing the most. Now if you'll excuse me, I gotta get my ass home." Erica acted as if she didn't know that Mikros concocted that story about her being pregnant to conceal what was really on his mind, but she could care less about what he said or thought. As long as she pulled the strings and motherfuckers moved like Yo-Yos, all else was of no importance.

Mikros went and sat at his desk, questioning why he didn't inform Erica that he knew she had some shady shit going on. Followed by him getting wrapped up in his own head. "Bitch you don't wanna play games with me," he said out loud to himself.

Chapter 20

8:17 pm Saturday night

Adonis, what in the world is going on with you? I'm not completely sure how you want me to respond to what you were saying about me staying at Tonya's house. I have the slightest idea about what's going on with you.

"Chaz you hungry?" Asked Tonya, cutting the conversation in Chaz's head short.

Chaz turned away from the TV. "Yeah, but not really. I'm just sitting here thinking about what my brother said earlier."

Tonya let out a slick laugh. "Girl when are you gonna cut the act." Tonya walked in front of the TV, wearing a half-cocked smile. "Ain't nobody stupid. I know Adonis is your husband." Tonya began laughing sadistically then suddenly stopped. "Who the fuck do you take me to be, huh? What, you didn't really think that I was just a stupid, naïve bimbo from the suburbs that couldn't put two and two together."

Chaz was totally caught off guard about how Tonya was coming at her. Where did she get the balls is the question that popped in Chaz head. Her disbelief had just reached its max.

"And then you had the nerve to come at me with that sideways game as if you were really some top-notch bitch. Oh please," Tonya waved her hand. "You ain't nothing but a prissy ass thot that thinks she counts for something. But sorry to tell you boo-boo, your husband couldn't get enough of this here South Jersey suburban pussy!"

Faster than fast, Chaz jumped up in Tonya's grill. "Bitch you!" Chaz shouted prior to swinging. Hitting Tonya with a swift stiff three-piece combination. *Boom, bam, pow.* Like a nigga cumming from a good nut, Tonya's knees buckled. Then she dropped. Granting Chaz the advantage to stomp a mudhole in her ass.

The first thing Chaz did was jump dead smack on Tonya's stomach. There was no reason for her to sympathize with Tonya's fetus. As far as she was concerned, the bitch didn't deserve the right to be carrying her husband's baby anyway. Like a raging bull, Chaz continued to kick, stomp and scream obscenities. Her fit of rage was in full swing. Chaz grabbed a small statue of some sort off the table and smashed it into Tonya's face, breaking the statue along with several of her facial bones. And had it not been for the impact knocking Tonya out cold, she would have surely screamed in agony.

Emotionally detached and unaware of herself, Chaz hurried into the kitchen to retrieve a meat cleaver. Apparently, she felt inclined to give Tonya an emergency C-section, despite the bitch only being three months pregnant.

Chaz ushered her demented self back into the living room with black hearted intentions. The abrupt thought of butchering Tonya into little pieces took control of her mind. Soft sighs and painful groans could be heard as the disoriented Tonya seemed to be regaining consciousness. Yet, undeterred by that fact, Chaz positioned herself in a perfect butchering stance. She stood over top of Tonya, raising the cleaver high. Suddenly and quickly she dropped it down on top of Tonya's stomach with authority. *Whack*!

"Ahh!" Tonya vociferated in excruciating pain as Chaz buried the hatchet deep in her gut. But the worst of Chaz pestilent actions were yet to come. Violently, Tonya flailed. Screaming at the top of her lungs. Chaz retracted the cleaver, attacking Tonya's throat came next. Silencing the bitch forever.

Breathing hard and heavy, Chaz stood up with Tonya's blood dripping from the hatchet. Casting a look of satisfaction, Chaz seemed to feel a lot better. "I hope you happy now. And to think I was really starting to like your little sexy ass," she stated calm as could be. When out of nowhere, a shitty grin took her mouth captive. With no mercy, she began to finish what she started.

Though Tonya was dead by this point, Chaz still took the liberty of delivering the undeveloped, now dead fetus. Apparently, she wanted the little motherfucker to come into physical contact with its killer. Chaz tossed the hatchet to the side before kneeling down and digging her bare hands into Tonya's stomach. With no regard for humanity, Chaz sat there literally pulling Tonya's intestines out.

Chaz disposition emulated that of a psychotic psychopath who giggled amusingly at her handy work. "Oh, wow. I know this ain't that little bastard's head," she stated admiring the decapitated head of the fetus. Chaz turned the head around in her hand, fondling it. The bitch had truly lost her mind. "I know this little motherfucker couldn't have been Adonis' baby. This little shit mad ugly," she stated hastily before smashing the baby's head into the floor. It was just barbaric of her to be behaving in such fashion.

Finally, the drama from Chaz's nightmare subsided as she awoke to the chaos of those ratchet huzzies from the reality show The Real Housewives of Atlanta. Then there was a strange thought that popped into her head. For some reason, she entertained the thought of suicide. She sat there on the couch needing to use the bathroom but declined due to her current state of mind. This was the absolute first time a thought like that came to her. So uncanny that it scared her.

Chaz placed her hand over her heart. She exhaled, "Fuck all that crazy shit, I gotta get things moving," she spoke to herself under her breath. She wasn't about to allow those crazy thoughts to gain momentum. Next, she moved to grab Dee-Dee's phone. Despite Dee-Dee being dead, her cell phone still served as a vital component in Chaz's next step. She opened the phone with Dee-Dee's passcode, then scrolled down the contacts until she found Monique's number. Convincing Monique to bring her the suitcase of money from Patty-Mae's stash, is what governed her next move.

I need you to do me a favor.

Chaz sent the text, then made her way to drain her bladder taking both phones with her. Before entering the bathroom, she spotted Tonya in the kitchen with her back to her. Lustfully, she stared at Tonya's fat ass poking out in the tan boy shorts she wore. "At least he ain't choose no busted bitch to fuck with," Chaz admitted to herself turning into the bathroom.

Tonya turned back upon hearing the bathroom door shut. She had been on high alert ever since her and Chaz had their little discrepancy over the fake bloody Tampon from earlier. Sleeping on Chaz was the last thing she intended on doing. Knowing that Chaz could flip out at any given time.

Just when Tonya turned back around to finish putting the steaks on the pan, her phone rung. It was a collect call from Adonis. She wasn't expecting to hear from him twice in one day. Immediately, she accepted. "Hey baby, what's going on?" she asked excited to hear his voice.

"Listen baby, I ain't got a lot of time to talk 'cause I'm supposed to be locked in right now. But dig this, I want you to get down here ASAP, so you could sit in on my arraignment Monday. Hopefully I'll get a bail low enough to post. But keep that between us, I don't want my sister stressing if things don't work out," he explained in an attempt to keep Chaz as far away from her uncle as possible.

"That shouldn't be a problem. I'll take care of it. I got you baby, trust me. I'ma make sure I be there." Her words were meaningful and full of commitment.

"A'ight, I gotta go love you!" Adonis spat then hung up in a hurry.

"I love you too." She rushed to express, but the call had already ended.

Chaz walked out the bathroom responding to Monique's text message, informing her of what she needed her to do.

"Chaz," Tonya called out.

Chaz looked up, directing her attention towards Tonya who was approaching the hallway where she stood. "Yeah, what's up?" Chaz responded in a low tone, tryna keep her not so fresh breath out of Tonya's breathing space.

"I got a lot of stuff to do tomorrow and depending on how things play out, I might not be back until Tuesday. Remember, I still gotta get rid of asshole's truck and all his stuff." Tonya told her as normal as possible.

"Girl I hope you ain't asking me to go with you. My brother specifically told me NOT to leave this house." Chaz dedicated more emphasis than necessary.

"No, not at all. All I was saying was I'ma be gone for a few days. Girl, you good right here. Do whatever you want," Tonya told her while shrugging her shoulders nonchalantly.

"Oh a'ight. That's cool with me. Just have my brother hit me up if he calls you." Chaz walked off getting back to playing text tag with Monique.

Tonya stood there for a moment, not really sure what to make of Chaz's carefree demeanor. Then concluded that the bitch was unique in every right. She rolled her eyes and smiled as she went back to the kitchen. Hoping and praying that she'd soon be with Adonis.

Mr. Ish

Chapter 21
6:13 am Sunday morning

The loud eerie sound of New York's cell door opening and closing could be heard echoing down the dreary corridor of the segregation unit. It's where he had been since the incident with Flex.

New York sat up on his bunk. He hated being in lock up. Even though it's where his sick ass belonged. Anyway, the nigga sat there wiping the cold out his eyes. He looked over at the styrofoam tray on the floor. After a few seconds he picked his breakfast up and sat it on his bunk. Then he took to the sink to adjust his hygiene. His morning breath was a demon in its own right. Wearing only his boxers, the middle-aged psychopath attended to himself as if he was actually normal. Upon completion of the task at hand, the six foot four, two hundred pound sicko hit the deck to engage in his early morning workout. Push-ups, sit-ups and twenty minutes of shadow boxing. Religiously, New York took pride in keeping himself physically fit, which was partly why Flex didn't have a chance at protecting his manhood.

Sweat beaded about his body something terrible midway through the workout. Nevertheless, his stamina and strength didn't seem to decline much. By the time he finished catering to his physical, he was drenched. In total, he did about five hundred reps of ground work and he threw about six hundred punches. Most of which was a series of combinations.

Again, he took to the sink to wash up. With minimum air circulating through the vent, New York's cell reeked of sweaty balls and nigga musk. Though, he was nose blind to his own odor. Once done, New York proceeded to consume the small meal tucked inside the tray. It was of a pathetic proportion. But never mind the amount, he needed to put something in his stomach. Leaving water to fill the void. He sat there in silence, listening to the sounds his mouth made as he ate. That's when out of nowhere, his mind began to travel. New York found himself in his childhood, pleading with his mother's boyfriend.

"No Jacob, please don't make me do that again!" The ten-year-old Tyrone cried. Jacob had been molesting Tyrone for about a year before he exploded. Although he had told his mother countless times what Jacob had been doing, she would never believe him. His mother would say things like, "Boy stop making shit up and sit yo ass down somewhere." But on this particular day, Tyrone's mother was nowhere around.

Jacob called lil Tyrone in the room to sit on his lap. Even though lil Tyrone had enough of being abused, Jacob insisted on imposing his will. Which was the wrong route for Jacob's pedophiliac ass to take. After all was said and done, lil Tyrone didn't hesitate to seek out his mother's .22 revolver and pump all six shots into Jacob's chest. That was the day lil Tyrone's life changed forever.

Immediately following the image of him pumping those slugs into Jacob's chest, New York's mind took him into the early years that he spent at the Crossroads Juvenile Center. In total, he was sentenced to eight years for Jacob's murder. And because New York spent the majority of his time committing acts of violence against the other kids, he ended up serving an extra ten years for sodomy and aggravated assault. Through the years of his incarceration, the nigga had become one hell of a whack job. At every chance he got, he was abusing the younger, weaker boys.

New York swallowed and smirked simultaneously. He really enjoyed reliving those moments. He scooped another spoonful of the cold oatmeal into his mouth. At this point, his mind started to recall the savage and brutal rape of his niece, Chantell. As he replayed that horrific ordeal in his head, he could feel his body chemistry start to change. Unmentionable things began to happen to him. Things that only a real live sick motherfucker would experience when having mortified images of something so gut-wrenching dance around in their head.

New York adjusted his hard on, throwing the rest of his food at the steel cell door. "I wouldn't be here if it wasn't for you!" he screamed in a rage in reference to Chaz. It was in that moment his reflection became his enemy. The sick nigga was convinced that Chaz was the blame for his present predicament. In his mind, if he would have never seen her face on the news, he would have never come to Atlanta looking for her. He could vividly remember the day he sat at home in his Harlem apartment as he watched the press conference on Fox Five News. The moment he saw her face, his world came to a screeching halt. All things subsided. "I'm coming Chantell. Hot dog it!" He clapped, jumping out his recliner. "Uncle Ty-dog is on his way," he yelled at the television as the Captain of the Atlanta Police Department continued to update the public about Chaz being a person of interest.

Twelve hours later, Tyrone-New York-Newsome was in Atlanta Georgia. Its been almost twenty years since the last time he seen his niece Chantell aka Chaz. And sure as horses are hung New York was hoping to get a hold of his niece before the authorities did. But due to the shady shit, her and Flex kept throwing at one another, it made it damn near impossible for New York to get a location on her.

Fast forward a few weeks later. New York found himself in cuffs after an anonymous tip led the Atlanta police to an abandoned house where he held a young girl captive.

In the present moment: New York laid in his bunk obsessing over Chaz. The psychotic bastard was in love with her. Well at least that's what his sickness led him to believe. However, it would be a volcanic eruption in Alaska before he got his greasy hands on her. Especially with Adonis now in the mix.

***

At the same time
In general population

Adonis was in his cell getting his work out in as well. Drenched in sweat, he punched on the makeshift punching bag. A punching bag in which he manufactured by rolling his mat up and ripping his sheet to serve as a rope to hold it in place. No bullshit, he was really working his hands and feet like a true professional. It was about 7:15 in the morning and he had been up for at least two hours. Going HAM on his conditioning was nothing short of who he was at the core. Bag work, sit-ups, push-ups, squats, and dips off the bunk. The nigga was really getting it in.

Breakfast had come and gone, yet Adonis still hadn't eaten. Although Erica had pulled a few strings to ensure that he got extra food, he still didn't seem excited about the incentive. Getting a hold of New York was the one thing he cared about more than his freedom.

Adonis threw the last of his blows. "Uh!" he grunted, pivoting away from the mat while unwrapping his hands. That's when his cell door clicked open. He was receiving a cell mate. The young brother took one look at Adonis standing there shirtless. Pumped and covered in sweat, Adonis gave the impression that being in the

142

cell with him was the last thing the young brother wanted.

The young brother's eyes doubled in size. He swallowed hard. There was no way he'd be taking his frail ass in that cell. About face, the young brother turned to go inform the C.O. he'd rather go to lock up than to be in there with Adonis.

Adonis found it amusing. He laughed to himself before grabbing his tray. His muscles were fiending to be fed. He opened his tray. It was packed to the max. He smiled, thinking to himself how good it felt to be blessed and highly favored, despite being locked up. Adonis closed and sat his tray down to wipe the sweat off and wash his hands. "Rec out!" yelled the guard over the intercom. Perfect timing, Adonis thought. He closed the tray, retrieved his personal affects then headed to the shower ridding himself of the filth that he accumulated over the last two hours became his short-term goal. Still exhibiting top notch militancy, he traveled down the tier in silence. Wandering eyes of other inmates depicted their admiration, as they stared in utter awe over the shirtless—hood version—of Captain America. Not to mention, the nigga looked like he was glowing.

"Damn! Y'all staring at that nigga like y'all want him to fuck y'all or something," blurted out one of the so called tough guys on the unit. A wave of defensive comments erupted in the air. It was evident that Adonis' body watchers attempted to protect their dignity.

Adonis paid the ego tripping bullshit no mind. Needless to say, he made it to his destination, handled his handle and went back to his cell to groom up. Once done, he had about twenty minutes left to use the phone. Calling Chaz would be his next move. It was imperative that he got all his ducks in a row. "Time to strategize," is what he told himself as he picked up the phone.

Chaz answered and accepted with the quickness. Finally, she was free to talk to her husband without the constraints of having to bite her tongue, whisper, or talk in code. Lord knows she was on cloud nine. "Oh my God," she began bawling from excitement. A flood of tears dispensed openly as her true feelings for her other half invaded without warning.

"What's up beautiful? You a'ight?" Adonis inquired.

Instantly, Chaz pussy got wet. She popped up off the couch with superhuman speed. Feverishly, she moved about to wiggle out of her spandex. Saliva secreted in her mouth. Her hormones were raging. "I will be once you give me that dick through this phone," she said now sitting down with her legs cocked open and rubbing on her clit.

Adonis gripped his wood. Her words promoted his body to react. "Damn! It sounds like you really miss a nigga," he replied with his back to the tier.

"Uhm hum," she purred, sucking on two fingers then sliding them back down to her sweetness.

He could tell that she was in the process of finger fucking herself. "There you go, tryna get your shit off at my expense." He laughed that sexy laugh she hadn't heard in years.

"You must really know your wife," her words were spoken in a sputter. Seizing the moment meant the world to her. For the past five years she had yearned intensely for her husband's touch. And even though Adonis wasn't exactly participating, Chaz wasn't about to let the opportunity of getting a good nut slip through her fingers. Literally!

Adonis began craving her in the elite of ways as he heard her pant, moan and purr through the receiver. Bricked up, he had to fold his dick against his stomach to prevent the obvious. "Let me know when you ready for me to speed it up, straight beat it up," he said just to give her a visual of how they use to rock. Especially when digging her out from the back.

Chaz began fingering her slit with exceptional speed while simultaneously tickling her G-spot. "I love you Adonis!" she yelled at the top of her lungs as she squirted out a mega orgasm. Adonis could hear the exhaustion in her breathing. He cackled to himself.

Moreover, he was just satisfied that his lady was satisfied.

Adonis stood tall to get a time check. Despite having a moment with his wife, time was still the enemy. Seven minutes till rec was over is what the clock on the wall read. But of course, the guards would be terminating all movements five minutes early. "A'ight, now that you done got that out the way, give me the war report," he stated.

As Chaz began to recoup, her awareness kicked back in. "Well, first of all Tonya hauled ass down to Atlanta like you instructed. The bitch so stupid she didn't even realize that I was going with the flow so easily. Anyway, you just make sure she does her part to get yo ass home. I got the cash to post your bond, but it's that heffah's credentials that should seal the deal," Chaz explained while wiping up the juices that flowed from her pussy.

"Word, that's what's up. Dig, they 'bout to call us in so I'ma call you back tonight. Oh yeah, and don't forget I'ma need you to enlighten me about this nigga Michael Owens. From what I heard the nigga some clown ass joker. A'ight baby, I gotta go. These country boys calling us in. I love you and I'll see ya sexy ass sooner than you can expect." Adonis' words were promising and filled with assurance.

"Of course you will. That's what I'm waiting on. I love you too." Chaz ended the call. She was now amped to death. Knowing soon she'd be getting her lover, husband, brother and best friend back.

When Adonis got back to his cell, the reality of being set free began to set in. But his freedom was still contingent upon Erica pulling through. Because even though he had no reason to discredit Erica for her word, he knew the biggest obstacle they faced was him killing New York inside the jail and getting away with it.

So he rationalized that he'd just grab the nigga up and break his neck. Quick and simple, leaving Erica to deal with the rest. Although in his heart he really wanted to make the nigga suffer.

Adonis formed a muscle and looked at his bicep, grinning to himself. He was amused at the mere thought of hearing the sick bastard's neck snap, crackle and pop. "Yeah nigga you might as well call me Kelloggs cause I'll soon be getting my Rice Crispy on," he said to himself grimly.

Chapter 22

Sunday Afternoon 1:14 pm

"Michael, I don't want you to worry about nothing. You gone be alright," Flex's mother said consolingly as she attended to the stitches in his rectum. Flex laid in bed on his stomach at a disclosed location, with only those that aided in his escape present. Neesha, Pike, his mother and Mikros. Yes Mikros!

After getting the full story about what took place with Flex, Sharon Owens contacted Mikros. She came at him something vicious. First, she ripped him for never bringing Travis' killer to justice, then for the suicide of Kliens. When it was all said and done, Mikros felt so guilty that shooting her some bail was his only vindication in lieu of a grieving mother. But what sealed the deal in his decision to help Flex out was the overwhelming evidence that clearly exonerated Flex as a murderer. Well at least for the murders of Patty-Mae and Teesha.

"Get that gay ass cop outta here. Y'all got that cracker looking all up in my ass." Flex blasted off.

Pike gave Mikros a bone chilling stare.

"Sharon, I'll call you later once I finish up with everything." Mikros expressed then left. He was nowhere near finished with what he started. He had so many loose ends that he really needed to tie up. There was just no way he was gonna leave Pandora's Box open. He had to cover all angles. Especially his own ass.

Sharon and Pike assisted Flex in sitting up before putting him in a wheelchair. Thankfully, the wheelchair was laced with a medical donut to relieve the pressure. Although his asshole was numb from the Lidocaine cream his mother put on his wound, he still felt major discomfort. "Uhg," he moaned as he sat.

"I got you bro, you good," Pike assured while helping him get situated.

Sharon motioned for Neesha to accompany her in the other room. Leaving the fellas to discuss things amongst themselves.

"Yes, Miss Owens, is everything alright?" Neesha questioned.

Sharon nodded her pretty little head up and down. The glee that glistened in her eyes spoke volumes. She tried to find the right words to express her gratitude, but nothing came out. Finally, about ten seconds or so later she broke her silence. "Yes baby, and thanks to you and Pike everything is fine." The emotions attached to her words were without parallel. The ladies embraced, sharing a hug of triumph in their victory of getting Sharon's only living son home to her in the midst of all the chaos. 'Cause she had for sure thought she'd never see Flex walk free.

"Ma!" Flex yelled, grabbing his mother's attention.

The ladies broke their embrace. Just as they did Pike appeared. "A'ight Miss O. I'ma see you later," he said rushing to give her a kiss on the cheek and a church hug. Without even allowing for her to thank him, let alone respond, Pike grabbed Neesha by the hand and ushered off. He had shit to do. Shit that Flex asked him to handle. And that shit was of most importance.

Mr. Ish

Sharon re-entered the room where Flex sat. There was no time for family bonding. None whatsoever. As a mother who sought to get even with the woman that has been a thorn in her side, Sharon was determined to get revenge. "Listen Michael, all I want you to focus on is getting better. Mama got this. Believe me baby." She smiled a mischievous smile. "Mikros done told me all I need to know." She cupped Flex's face. "And you can bet your ass that floozie Chaz gone pay."

Flex tilted his head to the side, looking at his mother with an uneasy feeling surging through him. The mention of him betting his ass psychologically played tricks on him. He felt as if Sharon was making fun of him. "Fuck you mean I could bet my ass!" His statement was scornful.

Immediately, Sharon realized she used the wrong choice of words. She stepped back. Sorrow dictated her expression. "No baby, I wasn't tryna be funny. I was—

"Yeah, whatever," Flex cut her off. "Get yo crackhead ass out my face."

Smack! Sharon slapped the hell out of him. "Motherfucker who the hell do you think you talking to like that!" she responded rightfully so.

Surprise took him captive. "Uhh," he exhaled like a broad getting penetrated. Never in all his years had he felt so soft, helpless and bitchified. Flex clutched his face, "Ma," he called out. Tears were streaming hard down his face.

Sharon waved him off. "Oh please, get your act together. You ain't got time to be sitting up here taking shit personal and feeling sorry for yourself." She began to turn up. "Now we gone figure this out together! We done been through too much and been apart for too long. You're all I got left!" She began to break down something awful. Out of nowhere she was bombarded with a slew of fluctuating emotions. For which she had no understanding of. There was no way to explain what she was experiencing.

"See! That's what I'm saying. You sit up here and start out strong and the next thing I know you fall apart. Just like when Travis got killed, you just fell the fuck apart," Flex stated uncompassionately.

'What a clown.' There he was, sitting in a wheelchair with his manhood stripped away. But had the audacity to be disrespectful towards the woman that gave him life.

"How the hell you expect me to trust that you gonna get that bitch Chaz when you can't even keep it together." Flex attempted to jump up and own his rant. But that gesture was short-lived. He collapsed, falling awkwardly on his side. "Fuck!" he shouted in anger. Blood could be seen seeping through the light green ball shorts he wore. Apparently, he busted a few of his stitches.

Instinctively, Sharon knelt down to help him. "Michael," she called out remorsefully. She went to help him up, but he spazzed and pushed her away. That's when she lost it.

Sharon got up off the floor wearing new skin so to speak. She had just transformed. "That's exactly why I should have left yo ass where you were at. You'sa ungrateful punk motherfucker. If you ask me, I think you wanted that nigga to fuck you in the butt." She got real belligerent with it. Cursing him out and attacking the little pride he had left.

Hopelessly, Flex sat there on the floor enduring the verbal lashing his mother bestowed upon him. And then the nigga started crying. I mean really crying. Crying like a baby wearing a shitty, soiled diaper.

"Wh-why you talking to me like that?" he questioned in a sob.

Sharon snapped her head back. Disbelief over his sudden melt down puzzled her. "Oh, I know you ain't just break down. Not you Mister 'Flex'," she chuckled. "Let me guess, you gave yourself the name 'Flex' because you so flexible in going from gangsta to girl. Nigga please." She was on a roll as she let out a high-pitched laugh. There was no holding back on her behalf. The way she emotionally detached herself from her firstborn was unheard of. Talk about tough love!

Still, Flex continued to fester in self-pity. "Okay a'ight," he begged... "Please ma, I concede. You got it!" he bellowed in submission.

"Concede!" Sharon jerked her head back again. "Boy please, you know damn well yo stupid ass just learned that word in jail. Let me guess, that's what you told Chaz uncle before he rammed his dick up yo ass!" Her words were torturous.

Suddenly, there was a shift in Flex emotions and characteristics alike. That newly discovered information filled his veins with fire and his eyes with destruction. But a small part of him was praying that he had misinterpreted what he heard. "What did you just say?" Flex's voice became deep and disruptive.

Immediately, Sharon wished she could take her words back. She knew she had just fucked up. The last thing she wanted to do was tell Flex that the man responsible for his life altering situation was the uncle of the bitch that set him up to begin with.

"First of all," Sharon said as she worked her hands with humble confidence. Which was a smart thing, 'cause regardless of what, her son was still as heartless as they came. There was no telling what he might do. So yeah, humbling herself at that moment counted for everything. "You need to get up off that floor and get back in that chair." Sharon bent down to help him up. Flex accepted her good willed gesture. And no sooner than their hands clasped, the monster within could be seen through the windows of his soul. Flex snatched his mother by the arm, pulling her hard to the floor.

"Ahh!" Sharon screamed from the abrupt impact upon crashing to the cold concrete. At which time, Flex made it to his feet. His strength was governed by his overwhelming desire to seek and destroy both Chaz and New York. Never mind the fact that he had just busted his butt back open. He could care less. Getting revenge was all his mind processed.

"Michael calm down!" Sharon told him as she strove to stand.

Flex felt the warm blood peddling down the back of his legs. He looked between them, his nerves began getting the best of him. Growing weak in the knees was the obvious reaction. He stumbled, grabbing the arms of the wheelchair for support. By this time, Sharon was up and at'em. His well-being was her only concern. She grabbed Flex to help him be seated. His legs shook uncontrollably as anxiety set in.

Sharon was just about to speak when Flex grabbed at his chest. Wide eyed, he took a deep breath. Apparently the nigga was having a panic attack. Confused as to what to do and how to respond, Sharon did the only thing she felt would help. Boom! She released a monstrous left hook to his temple. Dazed, his head began to spin. Yet his panic attack ceased to exist.

Sharon stepped to the side, giving Flex room to collect himself. "Listen Michael," her tone was sensitive in nature. She approached and kneeled at his side. "Baby there's a lot you don't know." She sighed. "Hell, there's a lot I still don't know." Sharon took his hand in hers, meeting his gaze. "But I'll tell you this. Mikros told me enough. And believe it or not that cracker gone help us out tremendously." An angelic smirk pressed upon her lips. She stroked Flex's face consolingly. "So let's do each other the favor of sitting our egos aside and let's get that bitch Chaz," she stated gruellingly.

Flex smiled, he was now feeling a bit better. Knowing his mother had his back made his heart warm enough to accept her proposal. "Ma, you already know. We gon' catch that bitch. And when we do, I'ma give her what she wants." He nodded, casting a deranged sinister look.

***

Meanwhile, on the other side of Atlanta

Neesha and Pike pulled up to where Flex instructed him to go. Pike parked in the driveway and hopped out, leaving Neesha in the car. Enduring the scorching heat wasn't exactly what she signed up for. But then again, whatever Pike said or implied she obliged.

Pike disappeared inside the dwelling he confronted.

"Damn!" Neesha expressed moving the sun visor over to shade her face. The thought of buying a better car flashed through her mind. She knew dog on well she was in violation of the black folk code, riding around in the summer with no air conditioning. Bitch lucky she ain't sweat her weave out.

Anyway, her phone rung. Of course, it was Mikros. Neesha rolled her eyes upon reading the caller ID. She answered, "Yeah what's up?" Her words were flat. It was evident that she didn't wanna be bothered with him. Especially since Erica had convinced her to play double agent. Leading Mikros to believe that she was willing to keep a tight lid on what it was they had going on. But when Mikros unethical shift in moral redemption went in the favor of helping Sharon and Flex, Erica insisted that Neesha keep her abreast of Mikros every step.

"I was just calling to let you know that you're in the clear to go back to work. And you owe me," Mikros told her excitedly.

"Ill! Fuck you mean I owe you?" Neesha was livid.

A sly giggle echoed through the phone. "Well let's just say I gave my Captain a convincing report," Mikros cackled.

Neesha gave her phone an ugly look. Cursing him out for being so fucking nasty and perverted was her first option. However due to her loyalty to Erica, staying poised over rode that. "Uhm, what a crying shame," she said almost in a whisper. Prior to her tone increasing, "I guess I do owe you." she agreed just to get him off the phone. At that moment Pike was approaching the car.

"Yes you do. But I'll call in that favor when I really need it. Toodle loo," Mikros concluded then hung up.

Pike popped the trunk, tossing in a black duffle bag, followed by him transitioning to the driver's seat. Neesha tried to forge a more welcoming expression when he got in but her disdain for Mikros was the deciding factor.

"Let me guess, you looking all crazy 'cause I had you sitting in this hot ass car?" Pike cocked a sideways smile as he started the car.

"Whatever. Drop me off at my place and be back by four 'cause I gotta go to work," Neesha replied in the midst of texting Erica the update.

"Oh a'ight, I see my baby got that clearance, huh?" Pike spat joyfully.

"Yeah," Neesha remarked bitterly.

"Damn, why you sound all angry?" he inquired, veering to get on the highway.

Neesha sucked her teeth. "Just drop me off."

Pike glanced over, "Aint dat what the hell I'm finna do!" he barked. Clearly, he took on her agitated energy.

Neesha responded by cutting the radio on. Arguing with her (PYT) Pretty Young Thug served as no consolation to her. It's not like he was the reason she was mad. It was more about her and Erica. Helping her besty was never an issue for her, but for the last week or so, her life had become an extension of Erica's. And although Neesha loved Erica, she was strongly considering pulling out while she still had her career, life and freedom.

Pike whipped up into Neesha's driveway. The gravel from the ground could be heard pervading the tires as he stopped short. Neesha had to brace herself using the dashboard. She cut her eyes, giving him a salty stare.

"Man look, I don't have time for all that attitude. Gon' get out and I'll be back to pick you up when you ready," Pike told her.

Neesha gave him a wrinkle face, then flipped him the finger before exiting. Pike crackled, then thought to himself, Bitch, you gonna make more than an ugly face when I slide this anaconda up in that ass.

By the time Pike got back to the honeycomb where Flex had been hibernating, his mind must of entertained a thousand scenarios of what he could have done with the seventy-five thousand dollars he had in that duffle bag. But none of those scenarios consisted of him giving Flex up and taking off with the money. Courtesy of his blood only pumping loyalty. Honestly, Pike was more so honored by the fact that Flex trusted him the way he did. On the contrary though, that still didnt excuse the young nigga imagination from running wild. Living it up and having fun to the fullest definitely flashed through his head. Besides those thoughts, Pike was no dummy. He knew seventy-five grand wasn't enough to live the way his heart desired. Let alone cross Flex over. Unlike most niggas pike age, he actually took pride in knowing that he held himself to a higher standard of being authentic.

After parking and grabbing the bag of money from the truck, Pike spotted Mikros' car. "Gay ass cracker," he mumbled to himself. Upon entering Flex's secret location, the pungent stench of stale blood could be smelled lingering in the air. Actually... the location wasn't really a secret. The old store front belonged to one of Flex's old flings. Although the place was closed down, it happened to be a pretty popular nail salon back in the day. But as it stood—the place served as Flex's hide out. Which happen to be a great spot for him to stay low key and out the way.

Moreover, the sour smell of —what the fuck— seeped into Pikes Nasal cavity. A familiar smell to say the least. Past experience taught him that a smell of that magnitude indicated a dead body somewhere in the vicinity. Furthermore, Pike was thrown for a loop. He was just there a few hours ago and everything was fine.

Cautiously, Pike approached the back of the premises, bag in his left hand, Glock .45 in the other. Although he couldn't make out any of the conversation taking place in the distance, hearing Flex's voice confirmed he was safe. Pike relaxed a bit, yet he kept his gun by his side. He heard a third man's voice. One he was unfamiliar with. Just as he was about to turn the corner, he was met by Sharon.

"Ohh," Sharon stated a bit surprised to see him.

Pike tucked the gun away. The possibility of a threat being present at that moment had just dissolved. "Hey Miss. O. Everything good?" Pike's concern and question was in tack.

Sharon shook her head up and down, "Uhm hum, yeah everything is good. I thought I heard you come in." She placed her hand on his arm and smiled after taking notice of the bag in his hand. "But things just got better," she told him as she led him to the back.

Up until that point, Pike was left in the dark as to what the endgame would be. All he knew is that Flex needed his help. And by all means he was willing to do his part.

The minute Pike reached the backroom his jaw dropped at the sight before him. Flex wheeled himself over to where Pike stood frozen like a statue. "I know you ain't tripping about that," Flex stated pointing to the corpse on the gurney.

"Naw, but I mean shit, what the fuck is going on?" Pike asked with a shoulder shrug.

"Let's just say I'm on my TuPac shit," Flex informed him.

Pike didn't understand. He wasn't a fan of subliminal messages. Especially one that consisted of a naked dead man lying on his stomach while Mikros and his Pathologist friend played in the dead man's ass.

"Yeah a'ight. Whatever the hell that means," Pike told Flex, handing him the bag of cash. BOOM BOOM... The muffled sounds of two shots being fired grab Mikros' attention.

Mikros drew his .40cal taking cover behind the corpse. As did the Pathologist.

Flex wiped the splattered blood and brain fragments from his face, "Damn, you could have at least let me get out the way," he stated wheeling away from Pike's lifeless body.

Sharon sat the long nose .38 Smith & Western down. It was still wrapped in the towel she used to suppress the loud bang.

Non remorsefully, Sharon hissed before saying, "You knew what time it was. You should have been on point." Her heartless statement was filled with conviction. It was obvious that she wasn't

Mr. Ish

even bothered by killing Pike. Why would she be, her primary focus was protecting Flex freedom. So when Mikros proposed that Pike become collateral damage to secure the safety of her son, Sharon didn't hesitate to sign up for the task. "Boy, nevermind all that." She waved Flex off. Roll yo ass over to that table and count out that man's money," she spoke in reference to the twenty-five thousand they had to pay the Pathologist for bringing them a body matching Flex's description

Mikros motioned for Sharon to join him while his Pathologist friend stitched up the dead man's asshole. They were really setting the stage to make it look like Flex was dead. And now with Pike becoming the corpse co-defendant in death, any reasonable person would believe that Flex was gone. But just to seal the deal, Mikros had one of his ex-boyfriends that worked for the Georgia Bureau of Investigation, to change Flex prints in the database. So yeah, in essence the nigga—Michael 'Flex' Owens—was presumed dead.

Sharon walked over to Mikros.

"Okay, listen," Mikros began to explain in his rare manly voice. "Here's the address to where the bitch Chaz is staying." Mikros handed Sharon a folded piece of paper. "From what I'm told she's driving a blue Buick Regal. The license plate number is also written down." Mikros went on to say as he pointed to the paper assuringly.

By this point in the conversation Flex had approached. He refused to let his mother and Mikros discuss Chaz without being a part of the conversation. No sir, it wasn't gonna happen. That nigga wanted to be apart of all things that pertained to the bitch who caused his heartache pain.

"Done!" exclaimed the Pathologist as if he had just completed a Rubik's cube.

In sync, everyone turned his way. The man's eyes danced nervously as the thought of joining Pike and the corpse became present. The guy swallowed hard.

"Alright dude, gather your things so you can be on your way,"

Mikros told the Pathologist, then looked at Flex. Signaling for him to pay the man.

The Pathologist moved faster than expected in collecting his belongings. The thudding of the dead body could be heard hitting the floor as the guy pushed the corpse off the gurney. Without a pause the Pathologist grabbed his money and hauled ass out the back door.

"Now that's what I call express service," Sharon joked.

Flex looked to Mikros, he had questions. "Yo Mikros, you sure this shit ain't gone come back to bite me in the—Flex stopped short of his words. "Man I just hope this shit works." he expressed bitterly.

Mikros sympathized, he knew the Owens family had been through a lot. His heart skipped a beat. "Of course it's gonna work. For one, we got no backlash from the dead John Doe over there. He was a bum that got killed by a hit and run. No one is gonna miss him. And with your boy over there." Mikros lifted his head toward the direction of Pike's body, "That only puts the exclamation mark on all of this." He smiled with confidence.

Sharon was about to speak when Mikros lifted his finger, pausing her as he answered his phone. It was Neesha, "Hey girlfriend, what's going on?" Mikros asked, putting his phone on speaker.

"Have you seen Pike, he was supposed to be here twenty minutes ago. I gotta go to work!" Neesha expressed angrily.

Mikros honed in on Neesha's P.Y.T. "Oh yeah." His eyes shifted back to Sharon. He gave her a wink. "Pike took you know who to get things situated for tonight. Remember what we talked about." Mikros said, alluding to a conversation they had about some frivolous shit he made up. Only to play into Neesha's game of playing double agent. Mikros wasn't a dummy by far. He knew Erica had Neesha playing both sides the whole time. He may have been a homosexual, but stupid he was far from. And boy were they about to find out just how smart he was.

"Yeah but how am I supposed to get to work?" Neesha questioned with attitude.

"Have you tried ordering an Uber?"

"Fuck you Mikros!" she scolded and hung up.

Mikros swiped his phone closed. "Okay, where were we." He slipped his phone in his pocket.

"You were just telling us about how we were gonna get this off without fucking it up," Flex stated, shifting in the wheelchair to get comfortable.

"I pretty much explained everything. Getting a new identity and disappearing is something you're gonna have to figure out." Mikros stepped into Sharon, he took her hands and pulled her close. "Sharon my darling," he reverted back to talking in a feminine tone, "I don't ever wanna see your little pretty ass again." Mikros cast a look of annoyance. "I believe I have done all I could to rectify the guilt that consumed me over the years. My deed is done. So, with that being said. Y'all enjoy your new beginnings." Although Mikros' words were heartfelt, his little spill was all the emotion and sympathy he had in him to extend. Not seeing them ever again couldn't come soon enough.

Flex grinned then held up the bag of money on his lap. "Don't worry about seeing us again. I got plenty more where this came from," he said braggingly.

Chapter 23

5:05 pm Sunday evening

Tonya's house

Monique parked Rep's Jeep at the curb in front of Tonya's house. Then she called Dee-Dee's phone but of course Chaz was the one to answer.

"Yeah, hello."

"Oh, hey Chaz. Can you tell Dee-Dee I'm here?" Monique replied.

Chaz began making her way downstairs. Just the mere thought of getting her hands on Pattie-Mae's money pushed her to think about being in Adonis' arms. She couldn't wait to get her man out.

"Dee-Dee went to the mall and forgot her phone. I'll open the door for you," Chaz told her with the biggest conniving smile.

"A'ight," Monique replied then hung up.

When Monique got out the Jeep she noticed that the Buick was parked in the driveway but didn't give it much thought. For all she knew Dee-Dee could have gotten a ride.

"Hey girl, what took you so long? Dee-Dee been beasting to get you down here to swing with us," Chaz stated the minute she opened the door. It was obvious that Chaz was hinting towards them having a Menajahtwa.

Monique's heart fluttered with joy. She so loved it when she was the center of attention. Hanging out with Dee-Dee and Chaz would most definitely fill the void of neglect from Rep's cold-hearted ass.

Prior to Chaz coming back to Jersey and re-uniting with Dee-Dee, it was Monique who often got called on to satisfy Dee-Dee's sexual cravings. True story. But never mind the past. As it stood, Dee-Dee was dead, and Chaz main focus was to use Monique's absent-minded ass to her benefit.

"Yeah, well, it's kind of hard to get away from that possessive ass nigga!" Monique lied, making it seem as if Rep was keeping her on lockdown. "That nigga don't let me breathe," she said, raking her fingers through her weave as she entered the house.

Oh, bitch stop the press, Chaz thought. Chaz knew Rep wasn't into Monique the way she advertised. Because unbeknownst to Monique, Dee-Dee used to put her on blast every time Monique called, begging Dee-Dee for advice on how to get Rep to treat her better. "I know that's right. Girl, that's what that good nah-nah do to them niggas," Chaz remarked while leading the way to the living room.

"Wow, I see you and Dee-Dee stepping y'all game up," Monique said admiring the décor.

Chaz plopped down on the couch, "Don't give me and Dee-Dee the credit, this some shit my brother worked out." Her statement screamed arrogance.

The reference of Adonis put a twinkle in Monique's eyes. She was definitely a fan. Every time she heard his name it was associated with respect. Not that the nigga was perfect. He was far from it and had his fair share of moments when he appeared to be weak and soft, but no one as of his current cypher could divulge those strikes against him, except Chaz. Which she'd never entertain the thought of doing.

"Uhm," Monique smacked her lips, "I know that's right. Shit, Qua and Rep was just bigging him up on the phone last night. Something about the social worker he was fucking," Monique expressed colorfully.

There was a pause in Chaz's response. At that moment, she knew Qua was still in the dark about his mother being killed. 'Cause there could be no way Qua and Rep could be in a prop given mood if they were aware. "I know them nigga's ain't cock sliding like that." Chaz depicted an attitude. She was never big on loud mouth niggas. "Anyway," she said changing gears. "Dee-Dee said she asked you to grab a suitcase from Ms. Mae's house. Did you bring it?"

"Oh yeah, it's in the car. I'll go get it." Monique got up to go retrieve the suitcase that held the money from Patty-Mae's stash.

Just as the front door could be heard closing, Adonis was calling Chaz on her cell phone. She grabbed it off the table, blushing upon taking notice of who it was. Hey handsome," Chaz said after accepting.

"What's good baby?" Adonis replied deeply.

"Nothing much. I'm just excited about tomorrow, that's all." Chaz's statement was filled with anxiety.

Adonis replied subtle and calmly, "It's gone be what it's gone be. But'um, what's up with that book you were working on. Why don't you tell me about it," he said, indicating that he wanted her to tell him about Flex and how all of her drama came about.

Just as she began processing the subliminal message, Monique was re-entering the house with the suitcase. Monique pointed to the combination lock on the suitcase and gave Chaz a —'what the fuck is this about'— look. Chaz grinned slightly and waved her off as she walked toward the kitchen.

"Oh yeah, you talking about that book I was writing. The one about the girl who they try to frame for murder?"

"Yeah, that's the one."

"Well it's basically about a young girl who had it rough growing up and bounced around the foster care system until she got adopted by a sweet lovely woman. And at first sight, the girl fell in love with her adopted brother." Chaz giggled shyly. "And he fell in love with her too. Everything was going good, they had really started to blossom into something special. As the years evolved, so did their love. He loved and protected that girl to the max. He taught her everything she knew. They even had their own language. But then he got locked up and the police took everything they had: money, cars and other valuables. The girl was left with nothing." Chaz's voice cracked as the pain of her past crept up on her. She sniffled.

Adonis could sense how hurt she was. His heart bled for her, he became angry.

"So, a little later on in the book, her boyfriend reached out to one of his best friends and ask him to look after his girl. But his best friend crossed him and tried to get with her."

"Hold up," Adonis broke in. "The nigga dead friend, I mean best friend was tryna fuck her?" That wasn't a slip of the tongue either. He had just informed Chaz that Mu was dead.

"Yeah," she replied in a low murmur, as if the truth of the matter was her fault.

"Damn baby, that's one hell of a twist," Adonis noted, implying he had no knowledge of the foul shit Mu was on. But there was no need to worry about his grimy ass anymore. Briefly an image of Mu flashed in and out his head. "Go ahead, finish." Adonis requested.

Monique appeared out of nowhere, "Bathroom," she mouthed. Not wanting to interrupt Chaz's call.

Chaz pointed toward the closed door off to the right, then continued, "So, the girl moved to another state where she and a friend got together. They started setting up drug dealers just to make ends meet." She paused, an image of Keemah popped into her head. "And that's when shit got crazy." Chaz was about to get into the thick of things, when commotion erupted on Adonis' end. She couldn't quite make out what all the noise was about, but she did hear a woman's voice. Then the phone went dead. "Hello, hello," Chaz called out, but there was no answer. "Damn!" she said under her breath before rushing to set the alarm on her phone to ring in twenty minutes." Alarm set, now this should be fun and easy." She told herself prior to joining Monique

Monique was sitting in the living room watching TV when Chaz walked in. Chaz scanned the area to get a location on the suitcase that sat by the end table. Mission accomplished, she thought. That was all she needed. The only thing standing in her way was the cell that housed her husband. And soon that wouldn't be a problem. But the one obstacle she didn't factor in her plan, was Flex. Cause as far as she knew, the nigga was still in custody and had no possibility of ever getting out.

Chaz accompanied Monique on the sofa. It was time she employed her manipulative tactics. Changing faces, Chaz's persona switched fittingly to accommodate her ruse. As always, she was on her conniving shit.

Chaz scooted closer to her prey. "Let me be straight up with you," she said, turning at an angle to face Monique. "Me and Dee-Dee wanted to know if you'd be willing to host an orgy that we're having here tonight. Ms. Mae was gonna have it at one of her spots, but we convinced her to have it here."

Monique's mouth dropped open. She was totally for it. She had heard so much about the slut parties and orgies that Patty-Mae was famous for throwing. There was no way she would exclude herself. From what she'd heard, every time Patty-Mae held one of her signature fuck-fest one of her girls ended up getting with a major figure nigga and selling pussy would become a thing of the past. Just the mere thought of what could happen was enough to get Hoenique to agree.

"Damn bitch, put your tongue back in your mouth," Chaz joked.

Monique didn't even attempt to hide her excitement. And the

hell with being all conservative and pleasing to Rep's unappreciated ass. This was her way out. "I thought Ms. Mae was out of town?" Monique questioned.

"Girl, Ms. Mae was in Atlantic City all that time. Gambling is like her biggest problem." Chaz moved the hair off Monique's shoulder then continued, "That's why Ms. Mae is throwing this little shindig. Bitch done fucked around and lost more than she intended to." Chaz finished up, cocking her lips to the side.

"OMG. I ain't know Ms. Mae had a gambling problem. But'um yeah, I'll be the host. I just hope I catch me a baller." Monique shot back.

Chaz smiled, "A'ight cool. Now all you gotta do is let me sample those goodies Dee-Dee told me about," Chaz raised her brow as a lure.

Monique squinted her eyes lustfully. "You ain't slick Chaz," she said playfully.

Chaz stood to face her. "Whatever do you mean," she stated, leaving out the living room on her way upstairs.

Monique just couldn't resist. Her inner jezebel was screaming for a few hours of freedom. "This pretty bitch pussy bet' not stink," she told herself shooting upstairs behind Chaz.

Crippled by way of awe, Monique stopped dead in her tracks as she sighted Chaz in the doorway of Tonya's bedroom. It was as if everything fell in perfect accordance. Starting with the complexion of the sun. Which cast the perfect lighting through the window. That contrast depicted Chaz to look angelic. Nothing was out of place. Her hair was beautifully untamed, framing her face with exceptional sex appeal. Complimented by her hard nipples pressing aggressively against the belly shirt she wore.

Monique instantly acquired goose bumps upon catching sight of the devious dame before her.

"So, I guess this is the part when you agree to letting me eat that box," Chaz stated just before sliding the tip of her tongue across her top lip.

Game on!

Monique couldn't help but morph into the avid sexual creature she was capable of being. The bitch lived for moments such as this.

Monique sashayed salaciously down the short hallway. She was trying desperately to match what Chaz brought to the table. "I can't wait to taste you." Monique uttered proactively as she got within kissing distance of Chaz lips.

Chaz responded with an intense piercing into Monique's hazel contacts. "The feeling is mutual," Chaz expressed breathlessly.

Monique went to speak, but her lips was met by Chaz's finger. "Shh, we wasted enough time," Chaz told her, then led her to the bed. Upon climbing on top of the mattress, the ladies didn't bother to delay any longer. In sync, their mouths began to collaborate, engaging in one hell of a kiss. Monique's pussy started to throb. Feeling Chaz warm tongue slither around inside her mouth appealed to her perversion.

Abruptly, the blaring alarm from Chaz's cell phone neutralized their passion. "Give me a minute that might be my brother," Chaz whispered in a breathless pant before hopping out the bed to get her cell phone. It was genius the way she made it seem like an incoming call. In a flash, Chaz began to rant and rave in dramatic fashion.

Monique sat there on the bed, utterly clueless as to what the fuck Chaz was yelling about.

"A'ight bitch, I'm on my fucking way!" Fake agitation held Chaz beauty hostage. She sucked her teeth. Then pretended to end the alleged call. "I gotta go pick up Dee-Dee and Patty-Mae at the mall. The Buick ain't got no gas so I'ma take Rep's Jeep," Chaz said moving about in a hurry. Monique started to object, but Chaz jumped back in, denying the possibility. "Now do me a favor and let my dude and his friend in when they get here." Chaz got close up on her. "And I'ma tell you something, both them niggas is fine as hell. So, if you gonna do ya little dirt I suggest you handle that before we get back," Chaz told her then quickly gathered herself to leave.

All Monique could do was cheese favorably. In her mind, getting her shit off without feelings being involved appeased to her in the best of ways.

"It shouldn't take me but a few hours. Them stupid bitches done got stranded in Philly. Anyway, let me go." Chaz shuffled out the room and down the stairs. Then she yelled up to Monique. "It's food in the fridge. Eat whatever you want," she screamed out while grabbing the key to Rep's Jeep off the end table. Followed by snatching up the suitcase full of money.

Moments later, Chaz was on her way to Philadelphia International Airport to catch a flight to Atlanta.

***

Fulton County Jail
About an hour earlier

Adonis had no understanding as to why the phone went dead. He had just started to enjoy his conversation with Chaz when the line went out.

Apparently, Neesha came to work with an attitude and decided she'd take her frustrations out on the unit. For one she was late, and most importantly, Pike had her car and she couldn't get through to him. So yeah, Neesha wasn't beat for the bullshit. Her attitude was on tilt. She hadn't even allowed for her notice of rec terminated to echo down the tier before flipping the switch from the officer's station.

Adonis stood tall, he was mad as hell. Chaz was just starting to get to the part about Flex when Neesha disconnected his call. He was livid. But at the same time he was programmed to deal with the stupid shit that came along with being locked up. "It don't matter, I'll catch that nigga," Adonis told himself as he glanced around the tier aimlessly.

Just then Neesha and another female co-worker entered the unit. "Lock the fuck in!" Neesha's voice stretched the distance. Nonchalantly, jokers lagged in their movements on their way to their cramped resting quarters. None of them seemed to respect her authority. Or the authority of any black sista in her position. But had it been a peckerwood-racist cracker, them niggas would have locked in five minutes early.

All but Adonis was slow to move. His steps were governed by confidence, walking as if he didn't have a worry in the world. Naturally, Neesha's attention was pulled in his direction. His demanding disposition wouldn't have had it any other way. And although the nigga was worthy of being gawked at for hours, Neesha wasn't pressed. Her mind was still wrapped around Pike's young ass. She couldn't believe he didn't show up to bring her to work. "I said lock the fuck in!" Neesha shouted.

Adonis hissed to no one in particular as the crowd of criminals passed the ladies on their way to their cells.

Neesha cut her eyes his way, then her mouth followed. "Yo, Mr. Flat Tire," she said louder than the chatter that milled about. Several heads turned her way, excluding Adonis. "Him. The tall guy," she said pointing.

One of the guys behind Adonis tugged on his shirt. Adonis turned around and acknowledged that his attention was being summoned. He gave the scruffy-looking shrimp of a man a 'fuck-you-want?' look. Not that Adonis was on some tough stuff, but he hated to be touched.

The guy dropped his stare. "The C.O. called you," he told Adonis looking away.

By this point Neesha was making her way towards him. "You gotta problem, huh?" she asked angrily while her partner strolled down the tier to secure the cell doors of those that went to lock in.

"Don't gas yourself. It ain't that serious." Adonis let her know as he stopped to face her.

Mr. Ish

"Who the fuck you think you talking to?" Neesha questioned boldly.

Adonis narrowed his gaze, nostrils flared, and his lips tightened as if he was posing for a photo shoot.

The thought and possibility of him jumping on her ass popped into her head. The bitch nerves were shot. Motivated by the wellness of her safety, Neesha radioed for assistance.

All Adonis could do was sigh amusingly. He knew what it was. He was about to take a trip to lock up. At that point, it took everything in him to restrain himself. The pressure of knocking her on her ass was steadily climbing. He was truly tempted to extend that jab, but hitting women wasn't his forte. "No Adonis. It's never alright to hit a female." The voice of his late mother spoke in his head.

"Wallace, what's going on?" inquired Neesha's co-worker as she approached. But before Neesha could respond the goon squad came filing through the door. "Get on the ground!" the leader of the pack yelled. Adonis kneeled, he was distraught. The guard rushed him, his crew followed. Within seconds they had Adonis in cuffs. A growl of frustration escaped him. Adonis was furious.

"I bet you ain't so tough now," Neesha said as the guards pulled Adonis to his feet.

Adonis collected a glob of saliva and spat in her face. That was like the worst thing he could have done. Those country guards jumped straight on his ass. Immediately, they took Adonis' legs from under him. Down to the ground he went. There was nothing he could do. Luckily, he was saved by one of the superiors. "Stand down! Stand down!" the Veteran Lieutenant insisted. There was no way that particular lieutenant was gonna allow that type of behavior to continue in his presence.

Once the thrashing ceased, they brought Adonis back to his feet. Despite it all, his damage was at a minimum. However, he did have a small gash over his left eyebrow. It was no big deal though. His wound would heal good on its own.

Neesha trailed the congregation as they escorted Adonis off the tier. Her face still promoted dismay. She wanted to cry. Getting spit on was the nastiest thing in the world to her. Yet, the bitch ain't have no problem with getting her face decorated with jism.

Anyway, it was protocol that Adonis be taken to the infirmary before lock-up. Although he suffered only a few bruises, he still had to be seen by a nurse and get the incident documented.

The lead escorting officer measured eye level with Adonis and out weighed him by a good forty pounds of muscle. Moreover, the thought of fucking Adonis up just to score points with Neesha crossed his mind. Subsequently, that thought had been voided upon taking notice that Adonis' eyes were dismissive of all fears.

Adonis took a seat as the nurse checked him out. She asked a few questions, put a liquid bandage over his cut and he was done. Afterwards the officer's proceeded to escort him to lock up, Adonis read the name tag of every officer present. He'd be damned if he let that weak ass beat down slide. Nothing got his libido flowing like getting revenge on those that violated him. He was gonna take pride in strategizing their demise.

The segregation unit reeked of mildew, shitty lighting and gloomy infrastructure. The paint on the walls were peeling and the muggy air seemed to compliment the setting. Such a perfect fit for those that were being housed there. Unruly banging on the cell doors began to ignite out of nowhere. It was customary for inmates in the hole to welcome the newcomer. All sorts of craziness were being yelled out. Half of which couldn't be understood. "That's right, y'all gotta real live one on y'all hands now." Neesha screamed, trying to incite more feedback.

"Bitch you gonna die first," Adonis spoke in his head with a smirk. Finally, they reached the murky, daunting cell. The thought of making things hard for the guards crossed Adonis' mind, but getting out that hell hole negated the notion. He was only hours away from moving on with his life. Monday couldn't come fast enough.

The C.O.'s went through the formalities of uncuffing Adonis and securing him in the cell. Afterwards, Neesha stayed behind. Initially, she planned to let him know that she was Erica's people and that him being taken to lock up was by design. But after Adonis' surprise attack, Neesha decided she'd give him a piece of her mind instead.

Neesha pretended to be busy with filling out the report regarding the incident until the coast was clear. She couldn't wait until her co-workers made their departure. Once by herself, Neesha stood at the slim window of Adonis' cell door motioning for him to approach. Her gesture was subtle yet convincing. Adonis started to flip her the finger and dismiss the bitch with a grab of his dick, but his awareness led him to consider that Erica may have been the catalyst behind his trip to solitary. In his own time, Adonis greeted Neesha at the window. Reading his face didn't take long. She could tell he wasn't receptive to her presence. Neesha kicked a note under the door. Adonis looked down. "That's not important at this time," Neesha stated bringing Adonis' gaze back to meet hers. Immediately, it became a staring contest. "You could give me that fake gangsta look all you want, but I'ma make sure I pay you back for spitting in my face, "Neesha professed with all the hatred she could recruit before stepping off.

Adonis never responded. He was never a fan of non-contact threats. "Only if that silly bitch knew I'd snap her neck," he mumbled while retrieving the note off the floor. "Erica," he said in his head as he copped a squat on his bunk. Pulling the tape off to read the note came next. The last thing he hoped to learn was that a problem of some sort had occurred. Thankfully, that wasn't the case as he soon found out.

Hey, sorry for the inconvenience, but it was the only way to get you and that sicko Tyrone on the same unit. He is in the cell to your right. Don't worry, my people will guide you the rest of the way.

Erica!

Adonis jumped up and shot to the door hoping Neesha hadn't left the unit. He desperately needed to see her. Knowing New York was right next to him made his blood boil with destruction. This was one of those rare occasions when losing control was appropriate. To no avail, Neesha was gone.

Once back at her assigned post, Neesha tried calling Pikes' phone again. It went straight to voicemail. Her level of aggravation began to quickly rise. Regret for even dealing with Pike began to settle in. Wanting and needing her car was what really had her stressed. And the conversation she was having in her head wasn't helping.

A fellow guard appeared as Neesha stared idly at the unit's security monitor. "Wallace!" he said.

She ignored him.

"Wallace," he called again.

"What?!" she snapped looking over her shoulder.

The guy looked at her weird. He had never seen her exhibit such attitude. "They're calling for you in operations. I'm here to relieve you."

"Relieve me?" she asked turning all the way around. Her tone was extremely nasty.

"Well listen, take yo ass up front and ask them what's going on. You could save your attitude for the next dude."

Neesha snaked her neck, snarling as she stormed out. When she got up front to operations nothing seemed out of the ordinary. She questioned herself as to who requested for her to come up front. Then she thought that someone was pranking her, which was a common theme among the guards at the jail. Pranking one another was their way of jailing to pass their eight hours.

Neesha was about to head back to her assigned post when one of her superiors called her to the side. Nonchalantly, the two took up space over by the water dispenser. The man began to speak, but his words were stagnant. "Neesha Wallace," A voice from behind spoke. She turned around, stumped. Her heart sped fast. Her breathing constricted. At that moment, she knew she was done. Erica stood before her with tears in her eyes as Captain Samuel Kelly and two uniformed officers advanced to take Neesha into custody. Erica stepped up, "I got it."

As the cold steel cuffs clinked around Neesha's wrist—Erica leaned in, whispering to her, "Request a lawyer. I'll explain later." At that point, that was all Erica could do to help.

Neesha was advised of her rights and carted off to the squad car that awaited her outside the jail. Betrayed, is what she felt. Embarrassment didn't exist. At least not at that particular time. She was more crushed and devastated over the fact that Erica was the one who took her into custody. But Neesha wasn't stupid either, she knew Erica wouldn't commit to crossing her independently. They were too close and shared too many dark secrets for this to be Erica's doing. Neesha knew it was more to it, but she would blame Erica for not protecting her the way she believed she could.

Crushed beyond expression, Neesha wore the pain of a thousand slaves on her face. Cloaked in silence, she gazed at the floor in the police cruiser as they transported her to the station. Her thoughts were absent, even though her mind was cloudy. It was just too much for her to process. Perspective is what she needed.

Erica and the Captain pulled up alongside the cruiser. They were following behind, yet neither mumbled a word to each other during the ride. It was nothing to be said. At least not on Erica's end. As far as she was concerned, the only tragedy in all of this was Neesha's arrest. Because the murder of Pike and the murder of who she believed to be Flex was of no importance to her. She could have cared less about any of it, as long as her home girl was good. But she wasn't.

In retrospect, Erica was actually glad that the call came in about Flex and Pike being murdered. That way she could focus all her attention on New York. That was the one thing she refused to let go of.

Erica helped Neesha out the cruiser. Nothing was said. The Captain told Erica he would meet her in the interrogation room then slid off. Upon escorting Neesha to the holding cell, Mikros appeared. "Sykes," he called out in a deep whisper. Erica turned around, fire dancing in her eyes. Keeping her cool was the hardest thing she ever had to do in her life. "Not now," she snarled and proceeded on. She knew Mikros was to blame. None of this would have ever happened if he didn't feel inclined to help Sharon Owens seek redemption for the pain and suffering she had to endure. Though the blame was to be shared between the two of them, taking ownership at that moment wasn't something she was prepared to do.

Mikros slithered his snake ass in front of them. "Wait a minute," he said in a masculine voice.

Erica attempted to keep it moving, but he stopped in front of her. "Look!" he stated loudly.

Erica sighed, "What Mikros?"

He smiled. "Well first of all, you can uncuff Ms. Wallace." Mikros looked at Neesha. He felt bad for her.

"Get to it Mikros," Erica insisted.

"Here's the police report that Ms. Wallace filed a few days ago reporting her car and debit card stolen."

Befuddlement took the ladies captive.

Mikros winked. "Yes, Ms. Wallace reported her car stolen earlier this week. And I have surveillance footage from the ATM of a young man using her bank card on that same day." Mikros held the reports he falsified out in front of him. Erica grabbed them, flipping through the back-dated reports. All she could do was smirk. She gave Mikros a sneaky look.

Mikros pulled out his handcuff key and uncuffed Neesha. "Sorry for the inconvenience."

Neesha screw faced Erica just prior to slapping the hell out of her. Swap! "Don't you ever speak to me again!" Neesha shouted then stormed off.

Mr. Ish

"Pike's dead," Erica blurted out, while rubbing her face.

Neesha stopped, her heart dropped. Sorrow, guilt and pain hit her all at once. She turned back. Tears began to cascade down her face. "No!" she screamed in disbelief.

Erica walked up on Neesha. Hugging her was the natural thing to do. Neesha sobbed, she couldn't believe that her PYT was gone.

"I'll meet you in the Captain's office," Mikros said. Leaving the ladies to themselves.

"What happened?" Neesha questioned in a sniffle.

Erica led her towards the waiting area of the station. They sat, hurt present in both their faces. It wasn't supposed to be this way. Neither of them had expected this. Erica started out by explaining to her that she received an anonymous call stating that there were two dead bodies in the back of a storefront across town. Then she went on to tell her that both men were found naked with their heads bashed into a bloody pulp. (A little something extra Mikros decided to add.)

Neesha's mouth was ajar. She couldn't believe what she was hearing.

Erica went on to explain to Neesha that her car was found parked outside the crime scene with Flex's county jail uniform in a plastic bag, in the back seat. Which was why she had been arrested.

Neesha's eyes got wide. At that moment, she knew it was Mikros. She knew 'cause she distinctively remembered Mikros stuffing Flex's uniform in a black plastic bag the day of his escape. Just then, Mikros appeared to inform Erica that the Captain was requesting her presence for the debriefing to announce the escape and murder of Michael 'Flex' Owens.

There was no reason to keep Flex escape a secret any longer.

"Hey Sykes," Mikros called.

Neesha cut her tear ridden eyes his way. Impulsively, she lunged at him. Erica reached to grab her, but she was two seconds too late. Neesha rushed Mikros, screaming in a rage. Mikros instincts kicked in. He drew his weapon. Yet, Neesha reached him before he was able to raise it up. A struggle ensued. Then there was the recoiling echo of three shots being discharged from Mikros gun. Two of which struck Erica, both head shots. The third one pierced Neesha's heart. Their bodies fell to the floor. Officers rushed to the lobby with their guns drawn. Mikros looked over at one of the first responders. "I have nothing to say until my union rep and lawyer gets here."

Chapter 24
Sunday night, 9:13 pm

"Bitch I wouldn't give a shit if yo momma asked to use my Jeep. Keywords 'My Jeep'. Yo raggedy ass better find out how the fuck you gone get my shit out of impound," Rep expressed theatrically over the phone to Monique. Rep had been struggling for the better part of the day to get in touch with Monique after receiving a call from the Philadelphia Port Authority informing him that his vehicle had been towed. But since Monique was waiting for Chaz to come back, ducking Rep's calls seemed like the appropriate thing to do. So after countless failed attempts to reach Chaz, Monique decided to answer Rep's call. Mainly because she feared that something may have happened and that Chaz reached out to inform Rep of it. Nevertheless, that wasn't the case by far.

"Well Chaz said she was gonna pick up your sister and Ms. Mae. I didn't know she was gonna get your car towed," Monique snapped back.

Rep was exacerbated. He didn't do well with shit like this. In his mind, bad experiences bred bad experiences. He took a deep breath. "I'ma say this one time, GET YO STUPID ASS BACK TO THIS APARTMENT TONIGHT OR DON'T COME BACK AT ALL!" Rep ended the call and immediately called back. "Let me ask your stupid ass a question, why the fuck you down in Bridgeton anyway? You told me Dee-Dee wanted you to bring her something."

"She did, she texted me and asked me to bring her a suitcase from the house."

"Yeah, but your slick ass didn't tell me she was two hours away. You made it seem like it was gonna be a quick run." The more Rep thought about the under-handed shit Monique pulled, the angrier he became. "Man... just get the fuck back up here or you gon' have to get your head out the impound," he punctuated then slammed the phone against the wall out of frustration.

Frantically, Monique proceeded to honor Rep's demand. Getting back to Jersey City was definitely in her best interest. She shot downstairs in search of the keys to the Buick. Presto! She finally found the keys in the kitchen on the counter. Then she grabbed a pen and a sticky pad to write out a note for Chaz. And still the stupid bitch believed there was an orgy waiting to take place.

Monique went to the living room to grab her bag so she could leave. Absentmindedly she realized the suitcase was gone, but she paid it no mind. It still didn't occur to her that she had been played. However, all that changed once she got in the Buick and realized the tank was nowhere near empty. That's when she took notice that Chaz got over on her. "Fuck-fuck-fuck," Monique yelled. Assaulting the steering wheel with open palms.

***

Meanwhile, down in Atlanta

Chaz checked into a rinky dink motel just outside of downtown Atlanta. The place was a real shithole. More so for welfare recipients, crackheads and prostitutes. All of which she didn't care about. Her main priority was to stay low key until she heard from Adonis. Everything was set. Patience was the only thing missing. Chaz tossed her fake ID card and hotel key on the nightstand next to the bed. She pulled off her green Bob-cut wig followed by her heels. Then the subtraction of her black sundress followed. Her inconspicuous attire was such a cliché, but her purpose intact. This was the shit she thrived for. Being adequately on top of her game was a skill she could have only obtained from Adonis. Leverage was everything.

Chaz quickly got comfortable in her nude attire. She so loved the flesh she wore. Next she jumped in the shower. There was no way she would allow for her man to come home after over five years in prison to some stank pussy. No sir, Chaz refused to stand for it. She would be sure to wash every nook and cranny of her exotic being. Making damn sure she detailed the spots she knew Adonis tongue, lips and hands would explore. That's when out of nowhere, indulging in a little self service crossed her mind. ASAP, Chaz exed the thought out her head and rushed out the shower. It was a no brainer. The last thing she intended to do was take away from the long awaited intimacy she craved to share with her husband. As she dried off she felt her stomach rumble. She was in such a rush to get things in motion for tomorrow that she hadn't eaten all day. "Pizza," she told herself.

After applying lotion and slipping into an oversize tee shirt, she surfed the web 'till she found a delivery spot and placed her order. Afterwards, she committed to going through the bag of items she purchased at the airport. She dumped the contents out on the bed. Most of it was hair products and cosmetics. Oh, and she copped an outfit from the souvenir shop. Being as though she didn't bring any clothes with her, that over priced shirt and pants was much needed. This was gonna be a new beginning for her. Which meant leaving behind any and everything from her previous life. Including all the chaos she had endured throughout Adonis' incarceration.

Reminiscence of how things began with her and Adonis probed at her memory cunningly as she shifted through the stuff on the bed. Physically she was present in that hotel room, but her mind placed her in front of the late Robin Davis. The sweet loving lady that rescued her from the horrific circumstances of her early childhood.

From the first day that Robin laid eyes on Chaz, she knew she would be bringing her son, Adonis, the little sister he had always wanted. Robin cherished the beautiful young girl she had chosen to adopt. But as the years progressed, Robin began to notice that Chaz and Adonis' relationship seemed to be more than that of siblings. She didn't want to believe it. However, the evidence was undeniable.

*****

Some years back

One day Robin returned home early from work and walked in on Chaz and Adonis having sex on the couch. Embarrassed, Adonis quickly gathered his clothes and ran upstairs. There was no way he could face his mother. For one, his respect for her was off the charts. Disappointing Robin was the last thing Adonis intended to do. But being a seventeen-year-young man seemed to get the best of him that day.

"Chantell, I can't believe you! That type of behavior is not allowed in this home!" Robin's remarks sent Chaz running upstairs bawling her eyes out.

Later that night, Robin insisted on having a talk with the two of them. She explained that sexual fornication was not permitted in her house. Then she went on to add that she forbade Adonis to be involved with Chaz in any manner outside of them being relatives. Reluctantly, the two of them agreed. But as always, Chaz was determined to be with the stud of a brother she had fallen in love with.

Weeks would pass, and life at the Davis' household had seemed to regain a sense of normalcy. Given the fact that Adonis and Chaz vowed that they would respect Robin's wishes, and if their feelings for one another remained intact, they would wait to see what the future held

***

Later that day

"Adonis!" Chaz screamed frantically as she ran at top speed to the basketball court. Her hysteria was quickly noted by all that was present.

Adonis was in the middle of shooting a jump shot when he heard Chaz scream his name. Instantly, he dropped the basketball and shot to her call of distress. Concern consumed him. With in seconds Adonis was kneeling attentively in front of Chaz. Her face obviously wet from the river she cried.

"Whats wrong Chaz, talk to me. What happen?" Adonis asked with empathy. He pleaded to get some answers, but Chaz was unable to comment. She was definitely in shock. Then finally she uttered the word mommy. And no sooner than Chaz spoke, Adonis was up and off toward the house. He didn't stop running until he reached his destination. With a cloudy mind and fearful feelings of the unknown, Adonis reluctantly nonetheless anxiously made his way inside. There was a still silence that loomed, only to be disrupted by the sudden scream from a young man who so desperately prayed that his mother was alright. Sadly enough though, Robin Davis was far from it. Captured by the Cobra Clutch of devastation, Adonis seem to have froze as he took notice of his mother. Awkwardly, Adonis' mother layed at the foot of the steps... DEAD!!!

***

Present Day

There was a knock at the door. It was the pizza delivery guy. Chaz dismissed her current thoughts and attended to the knocking. She had just been reminded that she was starving and had a thing for extra meat pizza. She could smell the intoxicating aroma through the box. "How much?" Chaz asked.

The delivery guy began to fumble the pizza box. He couldn't believe who stood before him. "Chaz?" he questioned in a low uncertain tone.

Fast as fuck, Chaz guard went up. She had the slightest idea about who the hell the pizza guy was. Her face drew a blank.

"It's me, T-Roy," the man stated.

Chaz jogged her memory. The only T-Roy she knew of was Adonis' cousin, and last she heard he was living with some fat white bitch out in the boondocks outside of Atlanta. Still, Chaz looked at him like 'who the fuck are you'?

"Aye gon' now," he smiled. "Here, this one on me." He handed Chaz the box of pizza. "Look'a here, I got some more deliveries to make, but'um I'ma get wit cha. And where da hell is AD at? I ain't seen that fool in forever."

That was the confirmation she needed. "Oh snap," Chaz blurted out. Tears of joy and excitement weld. She wiped them aside. "T-Roy!" she whined, overwhelmed by disbelief. Finally, Chaz had reconnected with a family member. Well kind of sort'a.

You see, back when Chaz first left Jersey and came to Atlanta, she struggled mightily to get a hold of somebody in Adonis' family. However, that served as mission impossible.

With no direction, address or correct spelling of any one's name, finding any type of next to kin became a full time nightmare. Not to mention, her sense of direction seemed to have disappeared. So yeah, Chaz was fucked in a multitude of ways. Largely in part why she had gotten her self wrapped up in all of that nonsense to begin with.

"T-Roy... Oh my God." Chaz reached out and hugged the short pudgy man. After a reciprocal hug, she pulled away. Clearing her face of the tears that fell. This was an emotional deal for her.

"Boy give me ya number. I'ma have Adonis call you tomorrow. He got in a bit of a jam, but I should be bailing him out tomorrow."

Chaz turned to grab her phone off the night table. By the time she turned back around, T-Roy was extending his hand, handing her a card with his number on it.

"Dis here is my bidness card. Me and my lady own da slaughterhouse down yonder. You have AD give ole T-Roy a call." T-Roy nodded then winked. "Tell cuz I got work for him."

Chaz accepted the card, the two exchanged farewells, and T-Roy was on his way. At that point all Chaz wanted to do was eat her pizza. She sat on the bed. That's when a slew of gratifying feelings instantly took over. She could finally see Adonis holding her in his strong arms.

Chaz tossed the crust from her third slice of pizza back into the box that sat next to her on the bed. Then she grabbed the remote to change the channel, stumbling upon the breaking news. It was reporting the unfortunate and accidental murders of Detective Erica Sykes and Corrections Officer Neesha Wallace. Intrigued, Chaz felt compelled to continue watching. And when the reporter stated that, "Neither tragedy was linked to the escape and murder of Michael 'Flex' Owens and his accomplice." Shock reared its ugly head Chaz had no knowledge of what the reporter had just stated in reference to Flex. Immediately Chaz grabbed her phone to fact check what it was she heard. And sure as shit stinks, that was the trending topic.

Chaz sprung to her feet, humming the melody to the legendary Biggie song, What's beef. She was really feeling herself. In rhythm, she tossed the suitcase on the bed. It was time she counted her money. What a glorious thing. She popped the lock: six-five-thirteen, was the combination. Then her face dropped. She was now pale. The suitcase was filled with boxes of tampons. In a desperate attempt to ease her devastation, she began a massive search of the missing money. Nothing! Except of course a sealed envelope stashed between the tampons. Her name was written on it. Chaz threw the envelope down and jumped up. Her heart felt like it was gonna explode. Her breathing increased drastically. "A'ight Ms. Mae. We ain't 'bout to do all this here. Make that money re-appear," Chaz stated pointing to the suitcase. Chaz closed her eyes tight, opening them slow as if that would transform the tampons to cash. Still there was no relief. Tampons it was. Chaz bottom lip began to quiver. Her emotional breakdown was well on its way. She was on the verge of losing her freaking mind. For some strange reason, she believed Patty-Mae's spirit was haunting her. Out of all the killings and cruddy shit she'd done since she was young, Patty-Mae's murder bothered her the most. Truth is, Chaz conscious was fucking with her.

Nervously, Chaz moved to grab the letter. She was really convinced that Patty-Mae's spirit was the culprit behind the disappearance of the money that her and Dee-Dee put in that suitcase. Then it hit her. Dee-Dee, she thought. Quickly, Chaz tore into the envelope subtracting the scroll. Then she got to reading.

Dear Chaz,

If you are reading this letter, nine times out of ten I'm dead and you're the one that killed me.

"So what bitch, who gives a fuck," Chaz stated disrupting her reading.

I know you probably saying so what and all of that. But I just wanted you to know that all I ever wanted was for you to be happy. Rather it was with me or Adonis. FYI, I been knew about him being your man. Shit, I was the one that snitched on his ass to send him to prison.

Chaz was taken aback by the newly discovered information.

Anyway, I thought that getting him out the picture would secure our relationship. And then you took off to Atlanta. Now I understand that Mu was on some foul shit, but truth be told we could have handled his little ass ourselves. But as always, your high yellow ass only seemed to be concerned with yourself. That's that light skin shit.

Well, let me rest in peace, while you try to figure out who you gonna cross next.

Mr. Ish

Deuces,
  Dee-Dee!

Alienated, Chaz sat On that motel mattress disconnected from all reality. There she was, the source of all her troubles. No where to go, no money and totally clueless as to what her next step would be. Fifteen dollars was all the money she had to her name, and that's only 'cause T-Roy gave her that pizza on the muscle.

However, Chantell 'Chaz' Davis wasn't about to stew in the misfortunes of her predicament. Making shit happen was what she was known for. Minor setback. Nothing major.

Chaz pushed all resentment towards Dee-Dee out of her head. She couldn't be mad. Nor could she stop laughing, which was such a Chaz thing to do. Rarely did she get played. After a few moments of amusing herself, she decided to clean off the bed and take it down for the night. 'Cause regardless of what, she still had Tonya as her ace in the hole. "I love you Adonis," Chaz said before going to sleep.

Chapter 25

St. Francis Medical Center
Trenton, NJ
Early Monday morning

It was the wee hours of the morning and the nurse had just finished administering Monk his medication. He had been cooped up at the hospital in Trenton every since Thursday evening. Obliged by the sucker shit Moss and his crew pulled. Yeah, they had really done a number on him. So much so, Monk had to be airlifted to the medical facility that housed severely injured state inmates. And boy was Monk's injuries severe: Broken jaw, fractured nose, three missing teeth, and to complete the job, his eyes were swollen shut. Though it was his ego and pride that endured the brunt of the beat down. It was apparent that his road to emotional recovery would be greater than that of his physical wounds.

The nurse emptied the syringe into the tube that protruded from Monk's arm. Within seconds, he was nodding out, drooling like a baby. Surely, he was enjoying his temporary escape to freedom, granted by way of the narcotics that invaded his system. Because in all honesty, getting high would be his only means of freedom in any shape form or fashion. Because still in all, his life sentence would forever remain in tack.

The other guy who shared the room with Monk hobbled over to get a good look at the man everybody seemed to take interest in gossiping about. Particularly because Monk's situation was rumored that Monk used to be the lookout while Adonis slung dick to Tonya. Although the rumor was inaccurate by all accounts, it still served as a great source of entertainment.

"Johnson! Get yo ass back in your area," the guard dictated with authority.

Mustaheem didnt hesitate to turn back and head to his bed area. Although he so badly wanted to finish what Moss started, he found great pleasure in keeping his composure. Knowing that his redemption would soon come. As far as he was concerned, everything and everyone associated with Adonis would soon feel his wrath.

"You act like I'ma do something to the nigga," Mu yelled back at the guard as he slowly climbed back in bed. And although most would consider Mu still being alive to be the biggest shocker thus far, there was one even bigger than that. The nigga only had three weeks left before he would be released. Considering the fact that he served majority of his eighteen-months sentence in the county jail. So by the time he got to prison he only had a couple of months left to do. And Lord knows that fool couldn't wait to touch down. Getting at Adonis or who ever was associated with him became Mu's full time obsession. His determination to catch up with Adonis and make him suffer like no other, had for sure reached his pinnacle.

Mu winced and grimaced distastefully as one of the staples in his stomach pinched his skin. "Adonis!" he growled while recapping the moments from when the swift response of the medical staff saved his life the morning he got stabbed up. And just like with the distorted facts about Monk's situation, rumors had sufficed that Mustaheem

Johnson had been killed. Moreover, Mu's motivation to secure another notch added to his body count was something that he refused to be deprived of. Starting with Adonis Abdel Davis.

"I ain't gonna fumble like you did. I'ma be sure to handle your your faggot ass," he told himself in route to getting as comfortable as his predicament would allow.

***

Flex's hotel room
Atlanta

"Now don't forget to call me when y'all snatch this bitch up! Here's the address and car info." Flex explained, handing a paper to one of the two niggas he had hired to track down Chaz.

Both men were known for their work in their respected field. "You got a picture of this broad?" Reef asked. Reef was a real live kidnapper. He specialized in child abductions. The nigga track record was no joke. Nine times out of ten, if a child came up missing and the parents was known to have a nice bank roll, Reef was more than likely the dude that grabbed the kid. At least in the Atlanta area.

Flex shook his head no, then stated, "Naw I ain't got one, but it shouldn't be hard to get. The bitch done been on every local news channel in the city." Flex wheeled himself over to the table where a laptop sat.

Reef looked at Goldy with a peculiar look. Goldy wasn't too sure if they should even be accepting the gig. Mainly because he didn't wanna get wrapped up in the extra shit that Flex had going on. Particularly, Flex's fake death and all that it entailed. Not for nothing though, it was the amount of money that Flex was dishing out that made the decision fairly easy.

Goldy shrugged as if to say, 'fuck it, it's whatever'. That was the beauty of having someone such as Goldy as a crime partner, the nigga didn't give a fuck. He was with whatever at all times.

"Here we go," Flex called out, grabbing their attention. The fellas advanced to see what Flex was talking about. It was a picture of Chaz that he retrieved from a news article online.

"Yo that's that chick Chaz. Man, everybody knows who she is," Goldy reported enthusiastically.

Flex responded with a tight faced stare. He took Goldy's excitement as a sign of disloyalty. Flex was about to commit when Reef erupted.

"Nigga stop acting like a groupie, Reef shouted then pushed his attention to meet Flex. We gon' find this bitch." Point-blank-period!"

It took a few seconds for Flex to rethink things. There could be no room for fuck-ups.

"Alright, here's ten racks." Flex handed each of them ten thousand dollars a piece.

The fellas thumbed through the cash, then sniffed it at the same time. "Word!" they said in unison upon their stare connecting.

"Now I'll give y'all the other fifteen when y'all bring that grimy, cum guzzling bitch to me!" Flex stated full of hatred.

"Say less my boy. We gon' have that hoe here faster than you can blink," Reef stated.

Flex blinked. "A'ight now, where that bitch at?" he remarked while looking around the room. Instantly, the three of them ignited in laughter.

At that moment Flex mother was awaken. "Michael," she called out as she sat up. Sharon looked at her watch. "It's five o'clock in the morning and I got a lot of business to tend to. I'm sorry, but you and your friends are gonna have to pick this up on a later date."

Goldy looked over at Sharon with that—'damn you look good for your age'— look.

Sharon peeped it. She blushed.

Flex peeped it, too. "Yeah Reef, I think it's time y'all go," Flex informed them clutching the Colt .45 under his thigh right.

Upon Reef and Goldy exiting, Sharon found it imperative to give Flex the rundown on how they were gonna maneuver their way out of Atlanta after killing Chaz. 'Cause as things stood, the both of them would be sharing life sentences if the shit was to hit the fan. But first they needed to get a different hotel room, 'cause Goldy was the one nigga that Sharon didn't trust.

Chapter 26

Monday morning

Fulton County Jail

Adonis tossed and turned all night. Repeatedly he'd found himself in rage mode. He tried everything he could to take his mind off being in the cell next to the sicko that snatched his wife's innocence. Nothing at that point took precedence over him sinking his claws in New York. And I mean nothing: Not freedom—Not Pussy—Not Money—Not NOTHING! That nigga New York had to go, and Adonis had to be the one to send him to his final destination.

The heavy keys to the cell doors could be heard kissing as they smacked against the guard's thigh on his way to acquire Adonis for arraignment. Adonis' case was scheduled for nine o'clock. However, the courts didn't waste any time with getting the accused to the courthouse early, only to have them wait countless hours before being seen.

"Davis!" the C.O. called, tapping on the cell window with the key.

Adonis lifted his head. His sleep deprivation was obvious. Giving the fact that he had bags under his eyes the size of lima beans. The guard took one look at Adonis and knew he needed backup. There was no way on God's green Earth that he was about to open Adonis' cell door without reinforcements standing at his side.

"Be ready in ten minutes. You got court," said the C.O. stepping over to New York's cell. "Newsome, get ya booty bandit ass up. You also got court."

Adonis could have sworn his ears deceived him. He shot to his cell door just as the C.O. walked off. Then he heard New York yell out, "Aight mister tough guy! Since you got so much to say, why don't you come up in here by yourself so I could give your asshole stretchmarks," New York shouted, followed by a sinistered laugh.

All sorts of revengeful feelings cascaded down Adonis' limbs. This was the moment he had been waiting for, for over twenty years. Every since Chaz explained to him what her uncle had done to her, Adonis could picture himself making the sick bastard suffer like no other.

"Thank you Jesus," Adonis mumbled full of excitement. Finally his prayers had been answered. It was just a matter of minutes before he got his hands on his prey. Assuming Erica had manuvered things in such a way for him to get away with murder before being released back into the free world. A smile of presatisfaction captured Adonis' expression as he stepped away from the cell door. There could be no way to describe the way he was feeling at the moment.

Simultaneously, both men began to correct their hygiene. Both eager, anxious and ready to get to the courthouse. But only one of them had reservations to leave.

Adonis thought about Erica and their agreement. His mouth watered. He couldn't wait to kill New York and then bail out to be with both his lady's. However, he would be crushed and devastated after learning that Erica had been tragically killed. But even with that monkey wrench thrown into the mix, he still had plan B. Tonya Jackson, the woman that was carrying his child. So yeah, favor and blessings still leaned his way.

Mr. Ish

The cavalry of guards that came to get Adonis and New York could be heard stepping hard towards the back of the segregation unit. There was much semblance between their strides and that of a choreographic dance routine. Both inmates took notice of the stomping feet edging closer their way.

"Newsome!" shouted the leading guard as he reached New York's door. "Christ!" the guard yelled, turning away from New York's cell door.

"Naw tell that punk ass C.O. with the pretty lips I'm ready. The booty bandit ready," New York screamed as he stood at the cell door naked while stroking his dick and laughing.

"You just earned yourself an ass whipping boy!" the racist white man remarked out of frustration.

The guards directed their attention to Adonis. Dealing with New York would come later. "Step back, turn around and interlock your fingers behind your head," the C.O. dictated.

Adonis complied. They moved fast, and within seconds he was cuffed and being escorted off the unit. Once again, New York had slipped through his grasp. But only for the moment.

***

By eight thirty, Adonis was at the courthouse waiting inside the bullpen for his court appointed attorney to come talk to him. His anxiety began to take on a life of its own. It was apparent that he wore his discomfort as a part of his uniform. He started to pace back in forth. Being in the dark as to how the State of Georgia operated in terms of abiding by "Law" and "Constitutional" is what bothered him the most. Praying only that he would be treated fairly and just. If there ever was such a thing for the black man. Moreover, a tall, slender, redhead woman wearing a cheap business suit entered the outside area of the holding tank. The files in her hand didn't look to be in order. She thumbed through them until she reached Adonis' folder. "Mr. Adonis Davis," the lady called out.

Adonis stepped to the bars. The woman's eyes grew wide upon

seeing the stud of a man who she called for. She was very much impressed with the physical attributes of the defendant she was to represent. *What a heartthrob*, she thought, forcing herself to look down at the folder she held. It would have been damn near impossible for her to not show her interest. Then she seen for the first time, a note specifying, "No Merit." She was thrown for a loop. She had the slightest idea about what the hell that meant. "I'll be right back, Mr. Davis," she said before stepping off.

***

Monday, 9:15 am
South Woods State Prison
Bridgeton, NJ

"Mason, you gotta report to Social Services. Your lawyer is here to see you," the C.O. said to Qua, pulling him away from his early morning phone call to Rep. "I gotta go bro. My whack ass lawyer here to see me." Qua hung up the phone in a hurry. He hadn't expected for his lawyer to come all the way from North Jersey to South Jersey just to see him. Usually, the motherfucker would send Qua something in the mail or set up a video conference. All of which was nothing more than false hope, uncertainty, and a bunch of legal terms that amounted to a subtle let down.

Qua went to his cell to retrieve his legal work so he could show his lawyer the loopholes he came across. Even though its been forever since he last seen his lawyer, he was always prepared.

Its been well over twenty months since Qua seen the stank mouth motherfucker that claimed to be working on his appeal.

Qua was directed on where to go. He entered the room where his lawyer was and tossed his legal work on the table. "What up though?" Qua's greeting was as ghetto as it gets.

The lawyer cleared his throat, "Morning," he replied in a parched tone, greeting Qua with his hand out.

Qua sat, slapping the lawyers hand away. He crossed his arms, advertising his dislike for the peckerwood that sat across from him.

"I don't even know why my mother hired yo greasy ass." Qua unfolded his arms. He was on tilt. "And don't hit me with that family history shit. I wouldn't give a fuck how much history you and my moms have." Qua wanted to continue but rendered it useless. He sat back. "Why the hell you come up here anyway, huh?" he added.

There was a small twitch in the lawyers neck area. He seemed tense. He grabbed the back of his neck, attempting to massage it. He stopped prematurely, getting comfortable served to be difficult. "I have some good news, and not—

"Good news!" Qua cut him off. "Motherfucker you better have spectacular news. I been waiting for a response on my appeal for mad long." Qua smacked the table.

The lawyer jumped. He had always been the nervous type. Which was why he chose to be a civil lawyer. But working for the late Patty-Mae and handling Qua's murder case was an exception. An exception that he seen fittingly. Credited to his secret sexual preference for transgenders. Which the late Patty-Mae was more than willing and able to accommodate. So in return, the peckerwood took on the role as the family lawyer, handling any and all endeavors.

"Well, that's what I'm here to talk to you about." The lawyer tugged on his shirt collar. Getting comfortable in the presence of a known killer was an obstacle he still hadn't conquered.

"Talk! I'm listening," Qua expressed folding his arm back across his chest.

The lawyer hosted a look of uncertainty. He wasn't really sure how to give Qua the good news of his appeal being granted, and the tragic news about the murder of his mother. He could still hear the echo of the Maryland State Police Officer informing him of Patty-Mae's murder ringing in his head. The disturbing news came so unexpectedly. Just the thought of having to articulate both highs and lows provoked the man to feel antsy. He must have played out a million scenarios in his head on how he was gonna break the traumatizing news. But there was no easy way to say it.

The lawyer began to finger fuck the folder he bought with him. Basically, he was buying time to construct some sort of subtle way to get it out. Then the deep rooted cracker within registerd. Figuring the only way to break the news was to be deceptive. A little family technique that his ancestors often employed back in the slavery days.

The lawyer withdrew Patty-Mae's life insurance policy, which pinned Qua as the beneficiary. Then he pulled out the appeal papers that quoted the amount of Qua's appeal bail. "Here you go Mr. Mason," he said with a sly grin. He slid the two stacks of papers across the table.

Qua leaned forward and reached for the documents. First, he grabbed the stack stamped, APPEAL GRANTED. Qua's face lit up like a jack-o'-lantern. Goose bumps of excitement ran up his arms. "Say word!" He looked at his attorney with the biggest grin any face could produce.

"Word." the lawyer replied with shifting eyes. Clearly he felt awkward as hell trying to sound hood.

Qua laughed while shaking his head. "A'ight, so now what's the next step to getting me out the fuck outta here?" he questioned.

"Well first we have to get your bail paid. And truth be told, you're not even supposed to be housed here in the prison. Effective immediately you're no longer state property." The lawyer began to unbutton his shirt cuffs and roll them up. "Now there should be no problem with paying your bail being as though your mother left you three houses and a healthy life insurance policy."

In no time Qua computed the statement. His face dropped as confusion embodied him. "Left me?" he questioned himself. "What you mean my mother left me three houses and some money?" Qua asked cluelessly.

The lawyer adopted a shocked expression. "You... You don't

know?" His tone became super sensitive.

"Fuck you mean I don't know! Hell no, know what!!!?" Qua shouted, immediately becoming hostile.

The lawyer took a deep breath. "I'm sorry Quaheem, but your mother was found dead down in Maryland."

"Naw man. My mother down in Atlantic City." Qua tried to smile. "I was just on the phone with my god brother and he said his sister and her girlfriend went to—

Then suddenly, Qua stopped talking. There was an awkward yet intense moment of silence. He smelled deceit. "When was my mother's body found?" he asked, able to holster his emotions for the moment.

"Well I got the call a few days ago. I'm not sure of all the specifics." There was no way that lawyer was gonna sit there and tell Qua that his mother had been decapitated. He made sure to allude that fact at all cost. The lasting he wanted to be on the receiving end of Qua's angry reaction. "But from what I've been told she had been dead for a couple of days. A week at the least," the lawyer expressed.

Qua couldn't cry if he had a gun to his head. The fury that filled him was indescribable. Immediately he began recalling the conversation he had with Rep earlier. And he could vividly remember Rep explaining that Monique was driving his mother's Buick 'cause Chaz used his Jeep to go pick his mother up, but the Jeep ended up getting impounded. Qua shook his head in disbelief. In a low hurtful voice he asked, "How did she die?"

The lawyer sighed. This was the most difficult part of their visit. He looked Qua in those dark evil eyes of his then stated, "She was murdered."

***

Courthouse
Atlanta 10:24am

Tonya sat front and center waiting for Adonis to come out and be arraigned. She had been there since the doors opened. Her and an older woman who was accompanied by a small child had been the first through the doors. Tonya struck up a conversation with the lady. She had more questions than the government. She asked about bail, payment options and she even inquired about what would be the most effective way to ensure Adonis would get a fair trial if it came to that. Covering all angles for the love of her life and father of her unborn child is all she cared about.

The judge sat behind the bench rendering bails to those that came before Adonis. Yet, Adonis' name hadn't been mentioned at all. Tonya was getting annoyed. She got up and asked the sheriff officer if Adonis' was on the list to be arraigned. However, she was instructed and directed to talk with the public defender. Not wanting to entertain the run around she seen coming, she decided to take a seat. Confiding in the older lady that sat next to her seemed to be her best bet. Again, Tonya struck up a hushed tone conversation with the lady after the judge ordered a ten-minute recess.

Just as she began bumping her gums her phone vibrated in her bag. It was Chaz. Tonya excused herself, giving the little boy a warm smile. The small child giggled lively. Once outside the courtroom, Tonya called Chaz back. She had just missed the call by a few seconds.

"Yeah girl, what's going on?" Chaz asked rather quickly. She was in no mood to be courteous. She needed answers about the status of her husband.

"Well, I been here since eight thirty this morning and ain't nobody telling me nothing," said Tonya.

"What? You been where, since when?" Chaz asked, fronting like she didn't have a clue as to what Tonya was talking about.

Tonya caught herself, remembering that she didn't tell Chaz that she was coming to Atlanta. But of course, Chaz already knew. "Oh yeah, I'm at the hospital with my grandmother. I thought I told you that Saturday before I left," Tonya wasn't good at lying or spinning the narrative. Being street savvy was definitely a missing element in her repertoire.

"Uh no, you left and said you were getting rid of ole boy truck. But whatever, did my brother call you yet 'cause I haven't heard from him?"

Tonya ignored the question and popped the battery out her phone, then went back inside the courtroom. She wasn't in the mindset of dealing with anything outside of the status of Adonis. She took her seat. Just then the judge reappeared and called for the next case. Moments later, Adonis was being ushered out in handcuffs. He scanned the audience, spotting Tonya instantly. He offered her a wink and a blew her a kiss..

Tonya's heart smiled.

"I love you," she mouthed with her leg shaking and pussy pulsating.

The sheriff officers walked Adonis around to the table where his attorney stood. The prosecutor stood to their right. The judge attempted to recite the case out loud when the prosecutor intervened. "Your honor, if you'd be so kind the State would like to request that this matter be rescheduled for next week."

The judge scrambled through his paperwork. "And the reason the State is requesting for a rescheduling?" The judge's question was legit.

"Well your honor, it appears that there is a lot going on and it's gonna take a few days to sort it all out."

"I hear you. But you still haven't given me a legit reason as to why I should reschedule an arraignment on a fifteen-year-old murder case." The judge unmasked his glasses.

"It's complicated."

Adonis' public defender jumped in. "Your honor, the lead detective on this case is presently being investigated in the tragic deaths of his partner, Detective Erica Sykes and her friend, a Correctional Officer named Ms. Neesha Wallace. So, as it stands I would like to move for an immediate dismissal of all counts against my client."

The stunning news of Erica's death solicited Adonis to feel sympathy. But the hell with Erica being killed. Adonis could only focus on his self. And an immediate dismissal was music to his soul.

"I'm listening," the judge replied.

Adonis' lawyer gathered her paperwork, reading from the notes she scribbled on earlier. "There are so many dots that are not connecting."

"Woe!" The judge stopped her. "Before you proceed, bail is set at two hundred thousand cash or bond. I'll let the trial judge sort out all the extras. Both the dismissal and the extension are denied," the judge stated then called for another recess as Adonis started to be escorted out.

"I'm gonna have you home this week. I promise!" Tonya informed Adonis as the officers led him to the back. Tonya turned to the older lady, "My baby coming home." Her face was consumed with relief.

"May God bless you and your family," said the lady as her and Tonya exited the courtroom.

***

Chaz and T-Roy sat in the parking lot watching from a far as Tonya left the courtroom. Following the dizzy bitch would be her next move. It was of high priority for Chaz to get a location on what hotel Tonya was staying in. She knew that if things went accordingly for Adonis, she could count on Tonya doing what's needed to be done in order for him to get out. But since Chaz had plans on killing her, she needed to be in the best possible position to achieve her goal. She wanted to make sure she was not jeopardizing her husband's release.

"T-Roy, follow that car," Chaz said after seeing Tonya get in the car with Sharon and Mack Jr., wondering who the hell Sharon was.

Totally clueless and unaware, Tonya had just hitched a ride and surrendered to being kidnapped. Unbeknownst to her, she had been talking to the mother of the man Adonis had killed. Sharon was sure to be at the arraignment, credited to the information Mikros had provided. And now with Tonya's stupid, absent minded actions, she had just given all leverage to Flex and Sharon.

During the drive, Sharon was elated. Shit couldn't have gotten any better than having the baby mother of the man she craved to kill in her presence. Michael gonna love his early Christmas gift, Sharon thought to herself as Tonya rambled on about Adonis. And boy was that motormouth telling it all. Tonya was giving Sharon an earful. Then out of no where Sharon damn near lost control when Tonya mentioned Chaz's name. The car swerved, Tonya screamed as she simultaneously braced herself. Mack Jr. began crying in the back seat. Sharon pulled over, she had to regroup. Just the mention of Chaz's name stirred her emotions.

T-Roy followed suit, pulling over about three cars behind them. Chaz's phone vibrated, alerting her she had a text message. She picked up the phone to read the message. "Shit!" she screamed.

"What's up cuz?" T-Roy asked concerningly.

Chaz looked at him with a face full of fury. "That crazy nigga, Mr. Ish just text me and said he'll finish the story in the next book 'cause he wanna leave the readers wanting more!"